Walking to Shenak

Carmelita McGrath

Also by Carmelita McGrath:
  Poems On Land and On Water
  KILLICK PRESS, 1992

Walking to Shenak

Carmelita McGrath

Killick Press
St. John's, Newfoundland
1994

© 1994, Carmelita McGrath

Appreciation is expressed to *The Canada Council* for publication assistance.

The publisher acknowledges the financial contribution of the *Department of Tourism and Culture, Government of Newfoundland and Labrador,* which has helped make this publication possible.

The writer gratefully acknowledges the assistance of *The Canada Council* during completion of this work.

Cover design by Vessela Brakalova,
Watercolour on handmade paper

∝ Printed on acid-free offset paper

Published by
KILLICK PRESS *an imprint of Creative Publishers*
A Division of Robinson-Blackmore Printing & Publishing
P.O. Box 8660, St. John's, Newfoundland A1B 3T7

Printed in Canada by:
ROBINSON-BLACKMORE PRINTING & PUBLISHING
P.O. Box 8660, St. John's, Newfoundland A1B 3T7

Canadian Cataloguing in Publication Data

McGrath, Carmelita.

    Walking to Shenak
    ISBN 1-895387-32-9

I. Title.

PS8575.G73W35 1994   C813'.54   C94-950005-4
PR9199.3.M34W35 1994

To my friends
who looked into storms,
and longed for pineapples

Contents

September 02, At Sea

I am on the deck of the M.V. Northern Venturer heading for Barker Inlet, Labrador, where I will teach anything except math. But on this calm sea, with this warm breeze and the high moon and half a million stars, I could be anywhere in the world tonight. Only the destination identifies this stretch of coast as north. I feel elated, as if the track of churned, moonlit water behind the boat is my whole past, the details being buried at sea.

I am sitting on a load of lumber. The entire deck of the Venturer is stacked high with building materials. Earlier, one of the crew chatted me up after winking at me all through dinner. "Where you going?" he asked, and I told him Barker Inlet. He pointed to a stack of rough wood, aluminium siding and roof shingles. "There's the addition to your school," he said. And then he got an attack of winking and told me he'd "check in on me" next time he got into port, just to make sure I was all right. Nothing could have prepared me for being single again, all the solicitude and lust, winking and staring. Four years with Derek, who always wanted to hold hands, kept me safe; if he were here now, the winker wouldn't even risk a glance.

I've been trying to figure out if I miss Derek. Maybe what I feel is an absence, a body part missing, half a conversation gone. Anyway, I'm going to forget about him. Derek, I am tearing up your last angry note and casting it into the path of the moon.

October 24

*Trapped here in frost and swirling snow, I remember the May after-
noon I bought this book I am writing in. It was a soft afternoon, and
I was looking for new poetry to read on a bench under the trees.
University was almost over, and I didn't know what I was going to
do with myself. Sometimes on such days on such benches I invented
other lives for myself—my romantic identities—poet and lover; this
was the season of gypsy skirts and contrived, piled-up hairdos. The
skirts hang in the closet now—the one where I keep my past—
chagrined and unironed and lopsided on their hangers, mute
evidence of the death of romance and the aching sensation I had all
last spring in my gut and groin. The sensation of being twenty-one.*

*I was looking for poetry, as I said, hopefully by a woman who had
given herself to love and adventure, someone whose strong, remembered presence would leap out of the words as I lounged on the bench.
Occasionally I would look up at the buds on the trees and the
passers-by. Or at the daffodils, having done their western tour in
February, turning up in St. John's now to grace our belated spring,
making us forget winter and all of our complaints and aching bones.
The buds on shrubs and trees were heavy, ready to burst with life,
lustful things. Purple and red and pink, full of sap, they seemed to
be engorged with blood and desire.*

*This is how I thought last spring; everything suggested sex and pos-
sibility; it embarrasses me now.*

I would look at the passers-by, and I would see in them possibilities for love and drama that they, with their closeted expressions and their nonchalance, did not seem to see in themselves. Sometimes when a particularly beautiful man came by, I would wish myself the courage to approach him, to tell him the story I had invented for his life, to invite him to become part of an adventure.

The adventure changed form with the weather, the seasons and the books I read. Sometimes there would be picnics on piers in the south of France. There could be laborious treks through the land of the Dalai Lama, a journey in search of wisdom. My own culture didn't present many possibilities; the age of exploration had given way to haphazard suburbs and dying communities. The landscapes I placed myself in were always foreign. Closing my eyes, I would bring the handsome young men with me.

During these moments, I would slip the finger with the ring on it away, hide it beneath the folds of my skirt; these moments of inventing lives for myself and for unwitting strangers were not good times to be reminded of an impending marriage, the need to find a teaching job before summer's end, or the coming school-year-ending marriages of friends. Sometimes I had the queer feeling that I would never see the "girls" again, for they would no longer be girls, and this belated spring would submerge itself in the sweat and tensions of a summer busy with weddings. Then we wouldn't be "the girls" anymore.

Sticky armpits in wedding dresses, arms waving goodbye. Hot headdresses and veils that needed to be carried by careful little girls. The smell of new perms in churches mixing with furniture polish and trapped heat.

Drunk on vodka slush at the stag parties, the men would think twice about what they had settled for in the way of jobs, but you know, she had a better chance of finding work there, too.

We were all embarking on that journey we call "going our separate ways"—not only a cliche but a misnomer, that expression, because our separate ways were all remarkably alike. Only the geographical destinations were different. Few went off alone; instead, two by two, like animals to the ark, they went off to start careers, families. They went to schools in small communities that were used to fall invasions of giggling young newlyweds sent to educate their children.

I took the ark by myself, so it's no surprise that I wonder a little about survival.

I don't know why I bought this blue book that day last spring, except that I found in the bookstore no volume of poetry by a woman who had given herself to love and adventure. Among the required texts and the self-help books and the Coles notes and the tired classics, I found no woman with that incandescence of spirit. Instead, the little book sang out to me from a shelf full of sad, stacked remainders. It had a pleasant blue leather cover, what my early life of shopping from catalogues has taught me is 'french navy,' and some gold

4

scrollwork, as if someone had been doodling on the spine in
anticipation of someday writing inside.

I noticed right away that it was just the size to fit inside a purse.
And, I thought, since there was no poetry to buy, who knows, with
all this fertile life around me, with the unknown adventurers strolling
beneath the trees, perhaps I could invent some of my own. A
heady prospect. Spring makes me dizzy, and ties words inside me
into knots until I get them out. Wind and sun excite me, make me
want to begin something.

This is not my first journal. I have always kept one, hoarding my life
in it, trying to make things happen by writing them down. Or trying
to pick sense out of the incomprehensible, or recording things it
might be dangerous to forget. And the man I almost married gave me
one once, but it had been large and heavy. It was a book that defeated
its purpose because, with its weight and size and flashy red cover,
there would be no chance of hiding it in the underwear drawer. It's
important for women to have somewhere to hide their writing; it's
an historical fact.

Derek had given me the book after a night in a bar where we were
drinking beer and trying to resolve, or at least talk about, some of our
differences. He was leaning over the table, close enough to me that
we could have touched and I, taking this for a conciliatory gesture or
an opening, started talking to him about the future, about how I
imagined it. I told him that I was writing more now, and that, in

the end, I couldn't see the two of us living in a small community, teaching for years and raising children there and building a house. I said that I couldn't stand the idea of the whole future laid out in front of us like an itinerary. I told him that I needed some mystery.

It was a garbled account, I'll admit. He shook his head after I'd stopped talking and remarked that it was probably because I was brought up Catholic, this desire for mystery, the wish to remove myself from a normal, sensible life, the inordinate weight I gave to the words of people I knew only through books. Perhaps it was the legacy of having heard too many Latin Masses and too many ghost stories, he said. Touching my hand, he told me about the real world.

Drawing on his own good sense, the unswerving practicality of his Methodism, he laid out for me the value of hard work. He said that I'd see, I'd be all right once I settled down. "Ah Sheila," he said, "children will do you more good than you could ever imagine." He always said that when he wanted to piss me off.

But later that week he surprised me with the big red book, its great blank, gaping pages expecting something more magnificent than I could possibly produce. I tried to write in it but stuck to my Hilroy notebooks when I had something private and unpopular to say, which was often. The big book still eludes me. Since I have come here, I have tried to write in it, but even now it contains a single entry, dated September 15.

Scattered snow all afternoon. Sky black. Curiously depressed.

6

The other day I consigned the red book to the closet which contains the girl on the bench. Sometimes from the closet, she sighs out at me, the perfume of memory lingering in her dresses breathes out into the room; she wonders when she will be set free again. I hardly go to that closet now. The other one is much more serviceable. It contains my new winter clothes, things I have never owned before, so padded and bulky that my way of walking changes when I wear them, and I remind myself of the child I was, lumbering around, sweating and losing weight from the exertion of trying to move in snowsuits. When I wear the stiff, shapeless things, I feel that I should have mitts sewn to my cuffs or a cap with knitted ears. I have to eat constantly just to keep up with myself on the cold days, but perhaps I will develop new rhythms that will slow me down, will make me capable of moving through snow as if through water, will give me a gait that will prevent the sweat from freezing into ice on my chin.

Today the wind reminds me of the wind in another, more familiar place. Schooldays in Herring Cove, before the mechanized plant, the paved roads, the modern bungalows with no steps coming down from their high front doors. I can see in my mind's eye the last leaves, cognac-coloured, smashed for trampling as each gale rushes in from the sea, leaving our yard littered with roof shingles and our windows covered with an opaque film of salt. And in this memory too, the shuffled march of schoolchildren in long cold processions behind horses and carts. This time of the year, I always think of those childhood funerals, the schoolchildren in their uniforms lined up to march at the end of the slow procession. There would always be old people who'd get to October or November, and then feel in themselves the impossibility of facing another winter. I can hear the teacher's voice, low but insistent, "Single file, children, single file."

Now I am the teacher. And, having gone from student to teacher so fast, I don't think I'm ready for it.

Here everything is different. Even getting used to the landscape requires something new of me. There are no trees with leaves to fall, only dark cavern-like stands of evergreens and eerie, rustling alders covered in dust from the road.

There are still the fall deaths. But here the old ones seem as strong as stone. The only deaths have been two young people. One was an accident, out shooting birds, a slip and fall down a cliff-face. The other no one says much about—a civil servant in another community, someone who'd been there for years, by his own hand. I have heard a rumour about embezzlement, but it's hard to tell. There are a lot of suicides in the north, so I've been told.

I opened this blue book with the intent of trying to record the curious feelings that came over me today as I sat behind my desk and watched the afternoon draw in around us like a tent. My students were working on a test, and the scratch of their pencils became loud inside me. I had the sensation that something awful was going to happen. But it was only a storm coming. No misguided plane crashing through the roof, lost in the snow; no word of disaster from the outside. Even the electricity stayed, the lights flickering and hum-

ming with static. Just the sense of something impending—snow in the linen closet, a dead lily in a spray of fresh flowers, a bird in the house. My heart thumped and, as I often had in childhood when there was something vague to escape from, I had that odd feeling that I was about to leave my body and float up to a corner of the ceiling.

I was going to try to write about that feeling here. Instead I have skirted it completely, circumnavigated my purpose and never arrived. I have instead recorded the history of this book, giving myself in the process a memory of last spring, a self-serving memory of warmth and possibility, one which deals with nothing, works nothing out.

The same thing happens when I try to write anything these days; I sit helplessly and lose my intention. The characters I invent become lost, and I can only deal with the real people and events around me, with lives that seem to me daily more curious than anything I could ever create. And then I go on a memory spin, escape. Sometimes I get a lousy poem for my efforts.

I will try to do it now, write out this thing inside me, the thing I have been avoiding.

The work roster says it's my turn to cook supper. It seems I can only focus on the weather coming down and what to do with two pounds of chicken.

Oddly depressed today. Felt like the classroom was closing in on me. Wondered what the hell I'm doing here. Storm whipped up northeast 3:00 p.m.

Walking home, lost my breath.

November 1

Lydia, one of my Grade Nine students, told me today she's quitting. I know that she's pregnant. She looks too small to have a baby. Everything I say to her now seems like an interference. I keep going to her desk, trying to help her deal with what she finds difficult. My hands trace the hard words with her, but I know that the books are receding. She is saying goodbye to them, her life already centred elsewhere. It is a useless thing I have been trained to do.

If a journal is going to be of any use, I should write in it every day — or at least often. Why can't I? Today — or tomorrow? — is the Feast of All Souls. In Herring Cove, my mother will be mourning her dead.

November, 13

The winter keeps drawing in, making the world smaller, and I keep opening this book to try to describe what it is like. But the pages are blank like snow; if I stare at them long enough, they become the outside world.

There is a lot of activity along the harbour; pretty soon the last boats will come and go and there will be no more until next July. I can't help but feel apprehensive when I think about this; it's a sensation in my throat, constricting, a dry lump. By next month, there will only be the planes. Rudy Connolly, who was here last year, says that in winter the planes sometimes don't get in for weeks. I don't know whether or not to believe him; he tells me about the bad weather and the isolation with such delight that I think he must be exaggerating. "There are days," he says, leaning over for emphasis so that his great furry hood falls over his eyes, "when to go out would be lethal. White out: you could be found on your own doorstep." Rudy tells me about sudden storms, hills of ice that rise unexpected on the winter sea, and about the 'sena,' which he pronounces 'shenak,' where the ice finally ends and the water and seals begin. He fancies himself a hunter, peppers his speech with Inuktitut he learned in night school. He likes the prospect of danger, that Rudy. But he's a man who's miserable about something, something secret. Unhappy people are the most dangerous.

Perhaps if I knew Rudy's secret, that would be something to write about. I need something. Because most of the times I open this book, I end up closing it without writing a thing. Locating just where I am and what I'm doing here seems impossible. The awful constriction in my throat can't be explained. Some days it's as much as I can do to go to work, and I sort of crawl home afterwards, laden with assignments to be corrected, some of which I feel will never get done. I don't really know how to grade the work anyway: some of the students are up to, or beyond, the material; others work as if they are groping around in the dark. The sky feels like it's pressing on my head.

Record keeping. What, after all, is the point of all these records? What do they tell? Certainly nothing of what is true. I mark my young people 'P' or 'A', but my entries don't give any clues about all the variations of absence or presence. Records don't tell about the endless, stupefying monotony that sometimes fills our days.

Yet we are besieged by Board and Government for more and more records, but they never ask, and the records never answer, why the students will probably quit before final exams from another culture arrive to demand their responses to such questions as why the automobile is so essential to modern society. I should write and tell the record keepers that the ceiling in the storage room leaks, and the precious registers are a sodden mess on the floor. And that we don't use automobiles here.

Perhaps the futility of writing anything down is what prevents me from recording events in this book. I could look at them later, in a year perhaps, and my words would only be like the skin on a pot of soup; I would have to skim off the events to see what's underneath. I would be underneath for sure, buried somewhere, but not too deep. Where in records is there a place to deposit premonitions? A way to record what hasn't happened yet, then edit it out, avoid it?

Still, I try to keep this clean. I try to write in sentences. These things strike me as important now, like dressing well no matter where you are, because some days it seems that, outside my work, the only words I speak are monosyllables, and the only things I express are agreement and hunger.

How are you, my dear?

Fine.

How is your work?

Good. Good.

And no problems with the students?

Nothing I can't handle.

And that is all I have to say most of the time; there is little point of saying much more.

I thought I had a lot to say in the beginning, and even more to learn. When Derek and I broke up, I'd already had the bug for adventure for a long time. Labrador, how it has attracted adventurers for hundreds of years! Adventurers or misfits. I had imagined myself, on that bright summer day as I signed the contract, as a brave adventurer, or at least a brave misfit. And there is adventure here, but do I pursue it? Have I got on my skis and trekked inland with a gun or a telescopic lens? Have I strayed far enough away from the house to get lost? Not a chance. Instead I have lapsed into a kind of stasis, a fish in thick weeds, not using up much oxygen or anything else for that matter. I don't ski. Don't skate. Don't like the cold. I was wrong. I had meant to go south.

But I have to laugh. Among the new people here, the outsiders, I think there are some people who thought that this would be a sort of

wild version of Banff. Like this one: a new nurse arrived last week
on the plane, bringing with her three sets of colour coordinated
ski-wear. Between shifts at the nursing station, between dispensing
pills and sewing up gashes and offering pre-natal advice that is
rarely followed, she can be seen heading up through the woods, a
bright flicker in assorted shades of pink and violet. Give her time and
she'll be like me, with her delusions filed in her compartmentalized
closets.

Through all this, though, I have come to see the one strong attraction
to this place. The attraction of otherness, a sensation that among the
unaccustomed, I might get to see things about myself more
clearly. I might figure out where it is I'm supposed to be. I can't help
feeling sleepy and already jaded but, the more jaded I get, the more
I want to push myself to some edge to avoid it. Not that I need a dose
of introspection, not that I like what I am finding out.

Last weekend I almost got into a fight with a fisherman from
Newfoundland who's missing his wife and thinks all women are
meat. Particularly marooned, single women. "It must be hard for a
girl like you," he said, squinting into my eyes, and when I got up to
leave the party we were at, he ran his hand along my legs and started
to slide it in between. I'd like to know what kind of feel he thought
he'd get through corduroy lined with long underwear. I turned on
him spitting like a cat, and I would have hit him if someone hadn't
held me back. There's an anger in me, waiting to bubble up, and
when it comes all I see is red. I don't know if the anger comes from

the incident, or someplace deeper. Looking back, I think I could have killed him if I'd had the chance, and was sure I wouldn't be caught. I'd better behave myself; teachers are supposed to be models of virtue.

I've got to write some letters tonight—I owe at least three. Introspection is bad for you, so says my mother and all of my relatives. It is not good to think too much about what's happening inside you; Uncle Richie said those very words as he rocked in his chair until the day came when he couldn't get out of it. My mother says that we are all worriers in our family, and we've got to take care not to get broody.

But getting into this letter writing business makes me feel that I am a missionary in China or something. Why not just pick up the phone? And what to put in letters anyway—the job and talk about the weather and desires for forbidden fruits like strawberries and pears. These are the things the letters I get are full of and they put me to sleep.

I had one letter the other day from a friend who's working in the Northwest Territories. "I'm going to make a bundle up there," she told me one night before she left, and then she looked ashamed. Her letter included the prices of all the junk food in the local store and asked me for a comparative account. Jesus! How much is a chocolate bar? This is what she had wanted to know after she had told me that Alan, her paragon of a new husband, had cast his eye on a student of his. Talk was going around. I don't know what Joyce expected; everybody knew that Alan had gone out with someone else a few nights before their wedding. She had told him, in tones of ringing bitterness that I can imagine even at this distance, that "he'd better get her soon because they age fast after sixteen." I can see Joyce shrivelling like a prune, stuffing herself with five-dollar chocolate bars, and demanding to know the price of mine.

"Joyce and Alan: Together Forever," the little silver and white wedding matchbooks had said. I still have a few in my drawer under the oil lamp, in case the lights go out.

And then there is Marina who, on her Central American odyssey, writes me about how her experiences are changing her, making her aware of the plight of people in other cultures, of how she may decide to change her life totally after this trip. I can see her making plans, trying to look like the local women, suffering her apartness reluctantly, blaming it on Daddy's money. I can see her in a sunlit square, wearing a long skirt of pure cotton, planning her whole life, waiting for letters from friends who have also had the gift of revelation — that life is too important to be wasting. I can't write her either.

The other letter I have tucked away against the day when I stop writing letters altogether. It will be the last one I respond to. It's from Derek. I'd thought I'd seen the last of his letters when I threw his bitter blame into the sea. I have started to see the whole correspondence thing as useless and — worse — a ploy, a way to never really leave anywhere at all. I have made a radical departure, done it alone. And, elsewhere, all my friends have changed. I might *as well leave them behind. It requires too much effort to keep the connections—and what for?*

Anyway, I brought too much baggage with me to start with. Four large suitcases, a trunk, boxes. Some of it seems pretty funny now, the stuff I thought I'd need. A swimsuit. Four fancy dresses. A large package of gift wrap? And then there's the whole summer of confusion and turmoil, the break-up with Derek, calling off the wedding. Time to jettison.

November 18

Today I took some of my students out for art class, although it was positively frigid. There was no wind, thankfully, and just enough cloud cover to make for interesting shadows. We were doing a collage of the landscape of the community; it now covers the back classroom wall, a collective effort made up of the work of all of those small, eager hands, so many visions gathered in pale blues and shades of white and stark black.

I think that I set up the project because I wanted them to see the community as I had seen it first, so I took them down to the docks and had them look at it as a new arrival would, coming by boat. "Eh, Miss, it looks so big," one of the boys said, sketching in a school out of all proportion to the one that sat there on the hill. Funny, just the opposite of what I'd thought, of what I had wanted somehow to show them, something that I perhaps could not show them unless they stood on the deck of a boat and entered my town on the south coast of Newfoundland. The smallness of outports seen from a boat. But how would they see my home? As impossibly big, perhaps, with seven hundred people and four stores and a take-out. I had wanted to show them how their community huddled there, so small and surrounded by such a large landscape. But they had seen it as vast.

When I arrived, I was horrified at the size of this place, how small it was, how different the air smelled, and how different the people looked, some of them already dressed in winter clothing although it was only the first week of September.

I shrunk back, and that is a secret I carry around, hoping nobody finds out, that I recoiled and wanted to leave, could not imagine staying, but the boat was leaving, its whistle telling me I had to stay for at least a week if I didn't get going right now, and it would be too late then—everyone would know me. My luggage was already ashore. A man at my elbow came very close, inspected me, then turned to his friends on the wharf. "New teacher," he said, smiling in a way that seemed to spread an infection of laughter along the whole group. Someone pushed me with an elbow, nudged me ashore toward the sign, "Welcome to Barker Inlet," and below this, an Inuit name, something from the time before the first European brought religion and diseases and imposed his ego on the very name of the place.

All of that came back today in a rush of memory—the night I slept on a load of lumber on deck and watched the Atlantic slide by in the moonlight, the great bottles of wine over which the new teachers, a baby-faced and enthusiastic bunch, all of us, had become acquainted, the curses of the crew as they kept drunken whites and drunken natives separate, avoiding some trouble I knew nothing about, the raw jokes people made when we lost sight of land.

Close to the centre of the mural we made today, one of the girls had pasted a cut-out figure of black cardboard, male or female, burdened by an unidentifiable load, trudging. I was amazed at how the girl had captured in a silhouette a stance, a way of moving, an attitude almost. Bent against the wind, yet somehow as strong as the wind itself.

For some reason the mural makes me sad. I'd like to have a place to be homesick for. But no place feels like home.

Inquest

"LOOK, if he was going to tell anyone about killing hisself, it would have been his grandmother. She's the only one he talks to, talked to." Amanda spits the last words out as if they'd been stuck, hard things like bones choking her and then, practically screaming, "Listen to me, will you, ask her, ask HER, ASK her!" But nobody is listening and Amanda's words fall on a wall of confused noise, the solid barrier of an event that has stirred up noises that make everyone incapable of listening. Perhaps the inexperienced ones had expected death to bring a silence—a pall, they say in books—so that the bearers of the dead become the bearers of the burden of silence. But here there is only a general hubbub.

In the corner by the curtain which separates the room from the rest of the house, Adela, swathed in skirts, sits rigid in a kitchen chair. She has already passed all questions and has gone into mourning, the only one who is silent. She looks at Amanda, her daughter-in-law, and shakes her head. Amanda's hair is loose and ragged where her hands all morning have been clawing their way into the pinned nest, as if pulling out reasons and explanations and meanings, each one more messy and incomprehensible than the last.

All of this offends Adela's silence. This is not proper. I will not speak, she promises silently, I will not speak. She inclines, extends her glass. Her son fills it for her and she leans back. I will not speak.

21

CONSTABLE BRIAN FARRELL is having a hard time with the confusion, not the least of it with the confusion in his gut, his stomach churning with acid and bile from the cups of black, instant coffee, from the rawness of this and the rawness of what he had seen this morning. No one will speak to him here, and he shuffles from one foot to the other, trying to gauge his position, trying to come up with a suitable demeanour, a way to elicit some response. But the only one who speaks to him is Amanda. And when she does, she screams, trying to threaten him, shaking her fist at him in an effort to make him interrogate the silent and inscrutable old woman in the corner. He would not, even if he thought it would do any good; he did not have the heart to pry into her thoughts about her grandson.

Six-forty-five am. A call at the tin can of a trailer that served as police station and lock-up. Someone had gotten up to go to the bathroom, and found—the voice on the phone trembled and fell. Brian was there five minutes later and there was the boy, horribly mutilated, part of his head gone, evidence on the wall that Brian could not look at, did look at, had seen, could see even now. Brian had gone outside and got sick in the snow, and the sight of his sickness had made him sicker still.

Meanwhile, there is a dead boy to attend to. Brian wants to go home to New Brunswick, or at least get a post stopping speed limit offenders and illegal moose killers in Deer Lake. He cannot get through another one of these, perhaps not even this one, without some kind of a break.

The hard thing, Brian thinks, letting the noise claim the room, is to find someone so obliterated, so obviously gone to the place where nothing, no one, can return from. In the sight of someone who has shot himself like that, there are no illusions about the sleeping dead, no attempt to find a pulse. Ricky has seen to the finality of everyone's experiences. He has left irrevocable witness. And no one seems to know why he did it.

No one is saying anything with the germ of a clue in it. Amanda is crying. Nobody heard the shot. The strangest thing, Brian thinks, is that nobody heard the shot.

* * *

AT the teachers' residence, they had found out about it first by
an early morning call, and then from the man who came to
collect the garbage, his face sorrowful as he held a bag by each
hand, the inappropriateness of him as messenger brought home
to the woman in the doorway.

"Did you hear...?"

"Yes," handing him two more bags and unable to say
anything meaningful or true or consoling. The garbage man
went away. The teachers had been having a party that night and
they would have to cancel it now. Funny, it had been a joke that
they had referred to the party, a party in one of the darkest of
months, as a party for "All Saints and All Souls." A "Bleak
November" party, they had called it, to cheer themselves up.

Today, nobody wanted to think about that but, in the queer
workings of the human spirit, the drive that makes people want
things to return to *normal*, people thought about it at intervals
during the day when Ricky's ghost did not hang like smoke
over their heads and must be off hovering somewhere else.
People wondered if the teachers would have the good sense to
postpone the party and, if they did, would they reschedule it?

* * *

AMANDA goes into the bedroom to be away from the men.
Joshua and his brothers are drinking. She cannot stand Joshua
when he gets like this, but she cannot criticize him. She looks for
Ricky in the closet and finds his hockey helmet and his sweater.
She strokes these. She cannot stroke Ricky because after all the
notes and information were taken by the baby-faced policeman
whose skin was as white as a sheet, they had taken Ricky to the
nursing station to wait for the plane. Ricky liked planes; when
he was about twelve, he had wanted to be a pilot. Amanda cries.
Why they have to take him out there and for what tests, what
evidence, she will never know. Everyone knows how Ricky
died. What they don't know is why. And they won't find that
out in a white room in Goose Bay or St. John's or anywhere else

23

for that matter. The last act of Ricky's lips had sealed them forever.

Constable Farrell wants there to be an explanation. His facts, no matter how hard he tries to make sense of them, are too paltry to add up to anything. Eighteen. Out of school three years. Unemployed. Good right wing. None of these things seem to add up to anything like a reason to die.

Amanda is sure that Adela knows something, that Adela has the key to Ricky's long silences. That she could say if she chose: this is how it happened, or, this is why he did it. Long after Ricky began answering Amanda and Joshua with grunts and silences, he had gone to Adela's, drank Adela's spruce beer and, as they had sat by the stove, Adela had tried to teach him his language. "Now that you're out of school," she'd said, "Perhaps I can teach you to learn something proper." So Adela had taught him Inuktitut, since Amanda did not care to. Amanda spoke Inuktitut only to the elders. Ricky spoke Inuktitut to Adela, trying it as he learned, and very little to anyone else. And who will Adela speak to now? But Adela may not speak at all; Adela has a reputation for being stubborn.

In Amanda's new religion, there is one God and the Devil, a great horned creature named Satan, and there are angels and demons of possession. Could Ricky be an angel now? But she remembers something that Mr. George, Jesus' messenger on earth in the Church of the Shining Kingdom, had said about death by one's own hand and condemnation. He had been concerned about the number of suicides, especially among the young, but his words had been little comfort to the parents who had lost children.

And where is Mr. George now, Adela wonders, why has he not come? She is one of his first recruits to the new faith. She had met him in the store one day, not long after she had lost the newborn girl she had tried to save by watching her night and day while the baby continued to lose weight. Mr. George had looked kind. "Let me help you put an end to your troubles," he had said, "Christ is waiting to shelter you in his loving arms."

But only Mr. Graham has come today, and he is of the other church. In the morning, he had drunk tea and put his hand on Joshua's shoulder, and left embarrassed, unable to break through the silence around the man who sometimes brought him fresh fish for his supper.

* * *

SHEILA cannot help thinking about the time Ricky had walked down the basement stairs when she had been sitting there drinking by herself in the dark. It's the way it always happens, she thinks, you forget minor events until the people who inhabit them somehow draw your attention, forcing recollection.

The sudden light from the opening door had made her drop her bottle, startled, and she was trying to retrieve it, cautious of possible breaks although she had heard no shattering of glass. It wasn't broken. He sat down on the steps gradually, hunching first, legs balancing him on the perch of his toes, and looked at her as if waiting for an invitation. "Hey, miss, what are you doing down here all by yourself? In your own house. Big crowd up there, half the town for sure. So what're you doin' down here?"

He hadn't really verbalized any of these things but she had thought that he said them, sending them out to her in something akin to radar, primeval communication. The unsaid becomes the whole point of the conversation, that's the whole problem here, she often thought, when she was carefully choosing her words, being the outsider not wanting to offend. Or it's one of the problems; it's the problem that puts me here right now, getting out of the way of potential arguments.

She had been talking to Dave Shiwak about education. They had been, in the most innocuous way, discussing her job. When Dave talked to you, he leaned real close. Women said that he was a ladies' man and was hanging on to every word in case you used the word 'yes,' and he was probably looking down your neck too. Sheila thought differently. It's a power game, she thought. He's waiting, she guessed, for the nuance, for me to trip myself up. He had asked her about her job and she had started, as she always did when she had to talk about teaching, by complimenting the children. "They are," she'd said, "the nicest children, tolerant of me, you know, after all, I'm just learning too, yes, really accepting and cooperative."

"Would you say, then, *complacent*?" he'd asked. "Maybe, you know, a bit too easy to get along with?"

"Oh no, no, certainly not, that's not what I meant," she'd responded quickly. "They're just very polite, that's all. They're not competing or rebelling all the time."

"That is nice for a teacher, I guess? Bet it's not like that everywhere, eh?"

"No," she'd said, "It isn't. Take it from me—it's a nice change." Dave had appeared then to be very deep in thought, his head bent even closer, brows knitting.

"Hhmn. Maybe it's something to think about. Perhaps they say 'yes' too easy. Maybe haven't got enough spunk. You know—of course you would, you're a teacher—they don't do as good on the public exams as kids even from small places in Newfoundland. They're nice for a teacher, I suppose, but for themselves...? I don't know. Maybe it's something to think about. Excuse me, I'll go get another drink."

He had been smiling as he went away and there she was again, trapped on a nuance, the ghost of a suggestion. He had issued her a challenge, a challenge involving the different words and hinted meanings and clashing priorities of their cultures. He had managed to suggest to her that the children were perhaps intimidated by these outsiders, the teachers with their odd assortment of accents, or that they did not complain because there was nothing relevant enough to complain about in the alien curriculum.

Waiting for him to come back with his drink, she remembers with embarrassment the content of the books she uses, where men wear suits to go to inexplicable jobs and women stay home making fluffy deserts if they don't go to the malls. There are always streets and drugstores and piano lessons. None of that exists in Herring Cove, not to mention here. But she feels that she is somehow an accomplice to that suburban view of real life.

She feels that somehow she should be doing better, that he has evaluated her and suggested that he doesn't approve, and that with the power he wields in the community, perhaps it would be better if she did not think her job secure.

Perhaps after all she does not deserve the gift of these children who are so good to her. Perhaps what is needed is someone with more experience who could make some real changes. All this he has made her think without saying a word of it.

And she had grabbed her bottle of wine and her glass and escaped to the dark basement where the only commentary was the wheezing of the ancient, asthmatic furnace. She sat on the steps and remembered, as she poured, that she had been told by a friend once that drinking alone was a sure sign of alcoholism. Drinking alone meant that you found conversation too much of an interruption of the real business at hand—getting drunk. It meant that you were building an intolerance of people, yourself included. When you'd rather just drink and have people stay out of it, her friend had said, you know you're in trouble. Her friend had spent her adolescent years at Alateen, trying to cope with her parents.

But I'm just looking for a little peace, Sheila told the furnace. I hate the way talk turns into arguments.

But she wasn't alone anymore. The boy, hand outstretched, sat on the step above her.

"Goin' to offer me a drink or what?"

"It's wine, you know. Do you like wine?"

"Not bad," he said, "wine. Sure."

"I've only got one glass and I'm not sharing it." She smiled to take the sharp edges off her words.

"Brought my own. Always come prepared." He held it up and drank the contents quickly and held it out for the wine.

The glass was cloudy and fingerprinted. "What did you have in it?"

"Whisky. Bourbon. Someone brought it."

My bourbon, she thought. "Quite a mixture you've got in there now," she observed, leaning over to pour. Sort of an

27

accidental, indigestible Manhattan, she thought. And all the unspoken thoughts hung in the air. What are you doing? What am I doing? They sat in silence, listening to the furnace, until he spoke and broke the heaviness around them.

"You need a new filter, you know."

"Who, me?"

"The furnace, I mean. I know something about furnaces."

"So you came down here on a mission, did you. To fix the furnace."

"I saw you come down here. That's why I came."

She could not respond to this, could not think of anything to say. Oh Christ, she thought, whatever I say, it's an opening. Something was expected of her, but what thing? What would happen next? Would he ask her if he could tell her something? Or would he tell her not to mind Dave? David's on a power trip, he might say, thinks he knows it all. It was a tactic that men used well, ingratiate yourself with a woman by calling the other guy a jerk or something.

Or would he, like the boy a couple of weeks ago, try to kiss her, tell her that she was beautiful. The other boy—how old was he, nineteen perhaps?—had said that, and told her that he thought she was 'classy,' and he had said it in a tone acknowledging that this was a statement he'd made after guessing what she might like to hear, a word that he would never have used if he hadn't been conscious that she was a little older and somehow different. She could tell that the word meant nothing whatsoever to him.

"You looked depressed. Kinda sad, like. That's why I came down. See, I'm kind of depressed, too. Right down on myself. Don't know why or nothing. Thought we could talk, you know, or something."

"I'm not depressed. What makes you think I'm depressed?" she found herself snapping.

"Yes, you are, miss. Don't mean to make a liar out of you, but you are. I saw it on your face. Takes one to know one. Looked like you were going to hit someone. Not me I hope," he grinned, "but someone. Or like—do something bad to your own self. Know what I mean? Like me sometimes I feel like leaving town and sometimes I know that that'd do no good, might as well, I think sometimes, leave the whole goddam shootin' match. Leave it all, go. But like Bernie, that's my buddy, he says to me sometimes, Ricky, you'd better stop that kind of talk or before you know it, you'll be bitin' the big one. Know what I mean? Ever think about that?"

"No, I don't."

"No?" He slurred the question. He was drunk, feeling sorry for himself.

In the dank cold, she had started to sweat profusely. The trickles ran like raindrops from her armpits inside the loose sleeves of her sweater, running in disconcerting rivulets down her sides. The sweater is cut loose, drifts away from her body, makes her feel naked. The sweat is like a secret bleeding. This was becoming intolerable, this painful drunk talk, the invasion of her quiet. She had no privacy.

"I don't know where you get your ideas. If you really want to know, I've never felt like that—*never*. I don't know what you're talking about. But I'll tell you what I'm sick of, Ricky, is people coming to parties and talking about death and depression and killing themselves. I'm damn sick of it. If you must know, I came down here to get away from all that. To be alone."

Even as she spat it out, she was conscious of the fact that her teacher voice had taken over, except that it was not her voice but the voice of her Grade Six teacher, the voice of a woman she'd hated, a voice filled with intolerance and feigned superiority and real malice.

Amid the dark stillness surrounding them, she heard his sigh of recognition, the soft sounds as he unfolded his long body from the stairs. Now would be the time to ask his forgiveness, to redeem herself, to cross space. Her Grade Six teacher was subsiding, yet there inside her, a malicious little voice was saying ' Oh, why bother, what does he know, he's only a boy, he's native, he doesn't know why you're uncomfortable, and besides, he's drunk, why bother?'

29

"Hmmn. Guess you're right. Don't have much to say, us. Sorry. I didn't mean it. Mistake. Sorry. I thought..." There was in those last words a long note of resignation and bitterness, but it was too late to try to have a real conversation with him now, to cross over those lines of age and training and culture and ethnicity, and privacy, for Chrissakes. And she didn't want to spend the night talking to a depressed young fellow looking for an ear. She wanted them all to go home.

The door closed. It was too late. He'd say she was a cold fish, a queer one, chip on her shoulder, drinks by herself in the basement. A shatter of glass brought Sheila to her senses, the broken wine glass on the floor, its shards gleaming in the little light from the small, dusty window, frail moon reflecting from snow to glass, sharp edges shining in a claret pool. She was at that stage of drunkenness when nothing makes any sense. Methodically, she picked up the pieces of glass, carefully, but she had to hold them away from her with meticulous precision as the largest shard, with a seeming will of its own, the broken arc of one of her favourite glasses, seemed to pull itself toward her arm, toward the pleading artery.

* * *

BRIAN FARRELL takes the skidoo and flies like a dart straight to Black Bear Pond in late afternoon with the sky like an indigo bowl around his head. The boy who died this morning was the same age as his brother Greg, six years younger than himself. At twenty-four, Brian feels ready to retire from the thing he used to look on as more than a career; it was a life in itself, one that removed him from the necessity of being poor, and from the prospect of long years of university study that he thought he wouldn't be able to handle anyway.

They sent the young guys here, guys big enough to break up fights, but still too young to be overly sensitive about death. Brian had seen a slide show in a training session; his vision of the north had filled with those images, images of white endless plains untouched by blood, of wild distances, of untold possibilities for a young man with a bit of daring in him. He had always liked the outdoors, liked hunting and fishing.

Afterwards, they'd been cautioned that it wouldn't be easy, that there'd be harsh... but he had already seen the clean, pure images and it was too late. Enamoured. The tools he had brought were a young, unflappable confidence and a gun. The first of these tools had quickly eroded, and the other had been useless from the start; what to fight with a gun when you are called in after a gun has already done its damage, a gun not unlike the one he'd bought for hunting, now used, finally, on the most trapped quarry of all.

Brian curses the sentiment that makes him think of Greg, wonder if he's all right, want to call home and check to make sure. Because all day, through the uncomfortable procedures of the task at hand, he has been comparing the boy to Greg, and this comparison has taken the young man out of the category of victim and made him someone real. He had tried to think in the terms of his job, the terms in which he talked to his superiors, but any voice of authority he had in him was drowning in the person of his young self, a cracking high voice trying to say, ...the victim...self-inflicted wound... 'wound'... a word so inadequate, the lie of it, 'wound' to describe obliteration. Or defeat. No words, there are no words to describe any of this.

He lets a yell, a scream, rip out of his body; it will not be heard above the engine out here in this empty space, and the sound which is unfamiliar to even his own ears is the closest he can get to the sense of obliteration he feels.

Like a shot fired in the dark, a sound that no one hears.

The yell clears out the troubled sick space inside his body, as if he has let go of a real physical presence, a parasite. Calm, he swings in a wide arc, and a halo of white powder shoots up and out in the glow of the rising moon. On the way back, his mind is free enough to think about a coming vacation, although it seems enough to let a little of the idea in, obscene to dwell on it.

Club Med. Sand and young women with easy lives and long hair, legs up to there. From now until then, it will sustain him, through tomorrow, a Sunday of uncomfortable silences, through Monday, a firearms safety demonstration at the school when all eyes will be full of questions, although no one will ask them.

* * *

IN her own house, away from Amanda's loud mourning, Adela positions herself in her chair with her glass and looks out at the stars. Twice this afternoon, her daughter-in-law came close to accusing Adela of knowing more than she would say about the chain of events that led Ricky to his silence. Amanda cannot forget that Adela did not encourage Ricky to go back to school when he quit, that when he talked as a young boy of joining the Armed Forces and becoming a pilot, Adela had thought that he was merely seeking an unlikely escape, a fantasy fuelled by television and comic books. It was a boyish dream uninformed by the knowledge that Adela carried, that you cannot escape from who you are, and she had asked him once why he dreamed of joining the cause of the military who were ruining their land.

Didn't he know that the Air Forces with their planes were flying along the very tops of the trees, disturbing people and animals, changing the traditional ways of his people in a way no one yet understood? The boy had sat and thought about that, and Adela was pleased. They had even had some interesting discussions, she and her boy; she had even been teaching him some of his language, though she realized that at his late age, his command of it would never really be complete. He'd never be comfortable in it. And now he was gone.

Things will be coming out in the next few days, Adela knows, and she will have to listen to it all, the 'what ifs' and 'I wonder ifs.' It will be said that he'd been in a few fights lately, as if boys died because they fought. The story about him and his girlfriend will go around, and the young girls will sigh and think about what love makes people do. And everyone will guess until their guessing makes them tired. Outsiders will say again how natives can't handle their liquor. Then something new will happen.

Adela is glad that the whisky provides a little numbness; it is a thing she has come to learn only later in life, and it has become necessary now that too much has changed and some things have turned completely upside down. Like the young dying and the old, the shell of herself, almost emptied of life, living on year after year.

Adela feels as brittle as the wind. She moves herself to the bed, stretches out in her clothes, pulls the quilt around her, tucks it underneath her body so there is no room for the wind. Only the whisky gives her body a liquid fire, puffs out the husk of her until her body lives. She looks out the uncurtained window, seeks her boy, searches for some trace of him in the high canopy of stars.

December 1

I have to put some things down in words.

I have decided to stay for Christmas.

*Some things must be put down simply to keep me from bursting.
What I really need is a good old friend for a long chat. Because I
have decided to stay here for the holidays with no good reason,
because, to tell the truth, I don't know where else to go. Sometimes
I play head-games with myself in the hope of spinning around in the
end, if not to an answer, at least to a sensible question. Should I go
home? Home? Where is home?*

*I left my parents' home too long ago, the very day I had a reason
to leave, and I've hardly been back for Christmas, or for anything
else, since. If I went back now, they would know that I am there because of the lack of somewhere else to be. They would know I've simply exhausted my possibilities. I don't want them to think they've got
any reason to feel sorry for me. They still don't understand why I
didn't marry Derek. They kept waiting to see who else was in the
picture, and when there was no one — well? They think Derek
dumped me because I was weird, and because I never could recognize
a good thing when I had it.*

*And they're used to me always running off somewhere. "You must
be some broke," they'd say, if I came home now. And I'd have to
listen to my father's criticism. My father believes in moving up in*

the world. One of his principles of success is that you never move to a place smaller than the place you came from.

No partner, no lover anymore, no time even to get a guy to bring home on my arm so that everyone would leave me alone, not before the holidays. A trip home, yes, would be a confirmation of the lack of something, an absence that would only worry the folks beyond their present state of brow-knitting. At any rate, it would be too typical to fly out, to be the young school marm out for Christmas, out of the wilds and with a new haircut, to leave and come back exhausted after two weeks of continual and convincing lying, of sitting stupefied by the woodstove in the new rec room where no one recs, of going cracked in the mall on a trip to St. John's, credit cards run sky high.

But—get a grip on yourself—what, after all, is there to lie about? Lie about, layabout.

I don't know, don't want to have to try to put a frame around it in my mind, yet I feel that I'm already making up lies in case I ever have to answer questions.

So, Sheila, what is it like, living up north?

In Newfoundland, it's both 'up north' and 'down north.' Either way, the question comes with an unstated instruction: tell me in twenty-five words or less. And if you've gotten involved in anything nasty, do us a favour and keep it to yourself.

Tell me...are you lonely up there, down there?

Answer: twenty-five words or less.

*What do you do for entertainment there? What are the locals like?
Are there Eskimos? Oh, yeah, how many? What are they like? Are
the youngsters in the school saucy? Have you met anyone? Do you
get depressed away from all your friends? Have you had any bad
colds? What kind of food can you get? Do you have enough warm
clothes? Do you need anything? Have you seen the northern lights?
Is your apartment warm? What are your roommates like? Are you
going back next year? Do you know? Why don't you do your
Masters—you can get a better job with your Masters, maybe even in
town. Do you write whassisname, or is that all over?*

*Tell me... why can't you answer? What's wrong? You seem a bit
touchy. There, there, now, have another piece of fruit cake. Did I tell
you about my leg — fell down in September, and it still hurts. If it
gets too much, you can leave, leave anytime you want. Come home,
sure, come home.*

*And I would have to see Angela in St. John's. Angela, my old best
friend. I've written to her during nights of drinking and depression
and insomnia. I have written to her, forgetting that we inhabit different worlds now, that I am not there to explain to her the context
of what I say. I have written to her that the seams that hold me
together seem a little frayed, that I am questioning a lot of things
and throwing most of them out, replacing them with nothing,*

leaving the hole gaping there inside me, coming up empty-handed but somehow freer, lighter.

So now she thinks I'm bushed and going nuts. I could tell by her last letter. And I've told her about the good times, the best parties I've ever been to, I tell her, so many of them. I tell her that I've been travelling inward and can now see auras around people when they're dancing. I forgot to tell her that was a joke, the thing about auras.

The one thing I really regret telling her about is how depressed I get sometimes. There's nothing really to do here but work and drink. Well, there are things, but I can't seem to do any of them. I called her under the influence and ended up crying on the phone.

She still sees Derek. He's got a new girlfriend. Angela got into graduate school — smart girl, she's not even going to risk getting bushed. She talks to Derek about me, but don't worry, she says, it's only because you are our common connection. We both care about you.

Her words are from out there. I don't know what she's talking about—common connection, what the hell is that?

I can't see her. And I can't go to St. John's because I'd have to.

December 6
Two teachers have left the coast. One had a total collapse, a nervous breakdown. She couldn't get out of bed. The other started

having visions, seeing God everywhere in the snow. The sparkles of snow and frost had become God winking at him. He's gone now.

These things didn't happen here, and nobody talks about it.

I did bring the damned subject up a while ago at one of our regular Friday night staff get-togethers. I was getting fed up because here it was—two of our colleagues elsewhere had lost it, a young man in our village had killed himself, and no one was talking about any of this. I mean, it had to have some kind of effect. I felt as if I were in the middle of a very skilful novel, where the one subject on everybody's mind is the one no one talks about. Not without prodding, anyway.

So there we were, surrounded by the weird and the tragic, and we were saying, "Oh, could you get me a couple more ice cubes while you're in the kitchen?" "Thanks." "So your new coat didn't fit? Where is it? Let me try it on. I'll buy it off you if it fits, cheaper for you than sending it back."

And everyone in extreme civility not saying a word about anything. A real parody of avoidance techniques. And in some ways it reminded me of home—don't talk about sickness or death unless you can joke about it, not in this house. You'll bring down something bad on us.

If it gets too rough, go somewhere, quit, will you, but stop talking about it.

Or like at the end of a mystery, go off somewhere and do the decent thing. Above all, don't make a mess. And don't talk about it.

At our Friday get-togethers, we also have a 'no-shop-talk' rule, which means that sometimes we don't say anything half the time.

So there we were, all of us in our Friday night best, scrubbed clean of our chalk dust, muttering the most banal kind of civilities. Or the most kind of banal civilities, however you want to look at it.

So I said, "Do you ever wonder about that guy George Barron, you know? And that girl—Tracy, was it? I met her on the boat but I never met George. Do you ever wonder, you know, what happened to make them so...desperate? It's only December; we have the whole winter ahead of us. But we seem to be doing all right..."

But I couldn't finish. Everyone had begun to stir uncomfortably, like my parents did when they first saw sex on television. In the silence, all I could hear was the scratch of corduroy pants on chairs, the sound of discomfort. Then Dave Marshall, who we jokingly call 'the sensitive one,' said, "Oh fuckin Jesus H. Christ, Sheila, you sure do know how to kill a party," and left the room, presumably to go to the bathroom.

Then all the stirring of pants on the seats of chairs stopped, and the silence grew heavy for a moment until it exploded into talk again. Dave had said IT! Dave always knows just what to say.

And I felt that from now on, it would be too easy to become a pariah, the evil messenger, bird in the house, black cat, the crack in everyone's sidewalk. I'd have to somehow redeem myself and become the carefree party girl I had been three months ago, or I'd be out in the cold with this crowd. Back then I'd had the sense to throw a martini party and look forward to skiing. I had danced around the living room until I was ready to drop, and had played silly games about what to take if marooned on a desert island.

Annie Peckham believes that it is through such games that one really gets to know people, although that's not why we were playing.

But I look around and think — no, this is how one really gets to know people. Watching their faces in a darkened room after someone has said something inappropriate. Watch them in silence, and faces will say both less and more than they mean. Watch how they move, squirm, avert faces and bodies.

Sometimes I think this is the only way that we are really getting to know each other at all. We're a strange bunch; we'd never find ourselves together anywhere if we hadn't all ended up here.

Dave Marshall serenaded us with a long flush, and came downstairs.

"That guy — George —" he said, looking hard at me, "was nuts before he got here. Otherwise, he wouldn't go nuts all of a sudden, would he? God sparkling in the snow—well, it's either he's a holy roller or he's done too much drugs, if you ask me. And Tracy Delaney—well, I knew her, a little bit, and I got to say this. No

offence to any of you girls—but some women shouldn't even think about coming up north. They can't handle it."

"Were you thinking about all that when you were up there on the toilet?" I asked.

But Dave had dismissed me; he's good at that. He turned to Rudy Connolly and asked, "Hey, Rude, still got that Murder Mystery Evening game? Who's up for it? C'mon, let's liven this crowd up a little bit. A little bit of murder is just what they need."

Now I have done it again. I was going to write about something else, but I've been travelling in the widest kind of circle until I am where I began; this blue book's spiral ornamentation suits its purpose well.

I wanted to write about that young man's death, because it bothers me.

But I'm too tired now.

December 7

That morning in November, a Saturday morning with a great brilliant sun flying high through scudding clouds. I was trying to sleep in; on Saturdays I rehabilitate myself from a week of mornings. I am not a morning person. I'm positively allergic to mornings, and the three or four coffees only kick in about two hours after I drink them. In fact, the only person I've seriously considered murdering earned that distinction by greeting me, pre-coffee, in a hall one morning with, "Hi, sunshine! Isn't it a beautiful day!"

On Saturdays I lie in bed and read if I'm awake, and I pretend to sleep if someone comes to call or the phone rings.

So that morning I was trying to hold out until noon, but there was a furious scraping out in the hall, as if some creature with brushlike feet was scurrying back and forth endlessly. My alarm clock said 9:00 am. Then it came to me out of the haze I was in that it was someone out scrubbing the hall floor. With a brush! It could only be Annie — she's the only person I know who would care so much about a rented floor.

Then the phone. I heard Annie's voice at a great distance, and I could picture her there in her rubber gloves, the brush dangling from her hand like some hapless caught animal.

The morning people and I live in uneasy truce sometimes, and I am aware that people who are purposeful on Saturday mornings are pissed off at me for not doing my share. Cleaning up for the party tonight, I thought. Tomorrow that hall will be so dirty our feet will stick to it. It'll smell like stale rye mixed with lemonade.

I had been noticing a bit of the compulsive in Annie lately, as if she is purifying her soul of some great weight through endless scrubbing, as if Comet makes her soul shine, and never scratches. I could tell her that she might as well wait until after the party to clean, when there will be a great and challenging mess for sure; the teachers' residence is a sort of communal property; people feel they have a right to make a mess. And we don't set a very good example.

Then the door, a gentle but insistent rapping. My door.

"Are you alone?" As if anyone would, could be here.

"No. I've got the White Fleet in here. Enter at your peril!"

And then the door opened and Annie stood there, the brush dangling from the end of a yellow gloved hand as if she had just surgically removed it from some poor creature she'd had to tell afterwards, "Well, we went in after the heart, but all we found was a scrub brush."

I was being silly, picturing all this, and was about to make a joke when I caught the look on her face.

"Bad news, girl. You know Ricky — God, I don't even know his last name—anyway, the young fellow who was over here with Gordon a couple of times. Well, last night he shot himself. He's dead. Nobody heard the shot. They found him this morning."

"Oh shit," I said, and then, blurting out before I could catch myself, "I guess that means we'd better cancel the party."

I was taken aback by my own reaction, as much as she was, but before I came fully awake and the news hit me, she'd already said, "Yes," in a flat voice and gone out the door.

All day I tried to apologize to her in different ways and attempted to explain to her as best I could that I didn't mean to be so callous, that the news had caught me unawares, that people threatened to do such terrible things to themselves that I couldn't quite believe them when they happened. At that hour of the morning, the whole incident had seemed surreal.

"Surreal...Mmm," she said cryptically. Like most people, she is elevated by tragedy. Tragedy always brings me down, turns me into a sort of desperate clown.

I didn't tell her what I was really feeling; I couldn't figure it out myself. I felt bad all day, and I walked around in a sort of daze, trying to picture Ricky in my mind so that I could give him the mourning he deserved from every one of us, so few of us in this small town. Yet although I tried all day to conjure him, and although he'd been in my house several times, just the week before his death to sell tickets in support of new sweaters for his hockey team, quiet, not saying much, shy; try as I might, I could come up with only two pictures of him.

He is at our place for a party, huddled with a bunch of young men his own age around the stove. I remember this because it got me thinking about how people stand around electric stoves now that most of us have moved away from wood heat, standing around electric stoves as if they gave off real warmth, a hearth custom, primeval, unchanged by the reality of the cold appliance. So there he is in my memory, hanging close to the stove as if it will warm him.

In the other picture, I am at the rink. It is after work and I'm watching a hockey practice for lack of anything better to do. I notice him because he is a fast skater, the kind who makes sparks with his

45

blades and sprays chips of ice behind his heels. I am a slow skater, and I watch in fascination as he zooms and turns and zooms again. So that in my mind that is how I remember him, his long black hair flying out from beneath his helmet as he barely touches the whooshing ice.

But I was cheating, just remembering that. There is another memory, only half there because I drank too much wine that night and a lot of other things happened. He'd come down to the basement where I'd gone with my wine for a bit of peace. He wanted to talk to somebody. He seemed down, but I didn't think much of it at the time. He started to talk about feelings. I've had a few of those chats with people when they're really drunk, and I didn't want another one. And he irked me because he had broken the spell of my privacy. I remember that I said a few words and sort of sent him on his way. Anyway, it's a night I don't really enjoy thinking about. That was the night I broke my favourite wine glass and felt like fighting all night.

Waiting for the Wind to Change

Wᴴᴇʀᴇ, tell me, does a woman go on a night like this?

Inside herself, that's where. Inside, inside, with intimacy, with a greater intimacy than she has devoted to all the previous rituals of the evening.

She has been outside herself, all around herself, around and around with the soft brush, with the harsh scrub, the gentle circling motions, the legendary one hundred strokes which will make her hair shine like Guinevere's. She has applied gels, creams, potions. She has applied depilatory and dark knowledge. She will have no superfluous hair and no superfluous time. There is no shortage of things to do; she can move, it seems, the ministering hands around her body for an eternity. After eternity, there is still the buffer and the razor.

Will this wind never let up?

She and I have a sacred pact, forged in the lights of bathrooms neither of us owns. We have witnessed our fair share of revelations. Like that night I sat on the toilet at Kibitzers when I looked down and saw her thighs, flattened like loose white slugs from the posture. They looked like the saddest things that had ever been abandoned anywhere, and I tried to caution her that we should leave now, since the revelation of those thighs would allow no satisfaction with the new lover waiting out there by the bar. I tried to teach her a cardinal rule: never have sex with a stranger when you're down on yourself. But would she listen?

Outside the snow is powder tonight. It's the kind that smothers me. I cannot see it, not here, but I can feel it. I catch her eye in the mirror. Her eyes are dark, black pools of a witch's well, bemused, distracted, and more than a little scared. There is a thing inside her that would go out into the storm. Thankfully, I have control over that.

In the mirror, I can see a confrontation coming, so I turn away. I know what's coming.

Outside the snow has reached the pitch of bedevilment. Out there, there is a party somewhere. She knows and she wants to entice me. Let's take, she suggests, this carefully nurtured body out there. Let's fill it with beer, with smoke, with wine, with food. Let's smother on that powder snow on the way there, drink in the busy air without fear. Maybe even fill this body with another body.

Ah, there's the clincher.

I am shuddering at how wrecked she came home from the last encounter. Pathetic. Her hair had been full of ice crystals forming, and her nose had dripped from the cold walk. The wet between her legs had gone icy, and her thighs felt raw and exposed from the sensations of hot, hot—then cold, cold. It had been too much for her or too little; it depends on how you look at it. I felt like crying when I saw that her blouse was on inside out. But did I question her, did I condemn her? No. I crawled into bed with her, slept with her, in her, told her that all of it was nothing to spoil a night over. I cajoled her into sleep with promises of change. I have not been able to deliver on those promises and tonight I worry.

From a distance, the wind carries us music.

What is the music that we hear, she prods me from the inside? Listen. For her, in every piece of music, there is a potential lover. The wind howls and I know that soon it will be midnight, after which she may grow tired, languish, stop bothering me to take part in the ritual of poisoning for which, she thinks, the ritual of purification in the bathroom has been only a rehearsal.

At midnight, the dogs begin their incessant howling. The

sound travels from the loneliest part of town where the dwellings begin, across the strip of houses by the government depot, past the shacks huddled by the wharf, travelling northwest, circling around to the better houses on the hill. We are in the middle of the circle, surrounded by the keening. On nights like this we have amused ourselves by wondering how the dogs know it's midnight, by attempting to identify their individual voices, by guessing what diabolical force might have placed our house in the middle of the circle. I am disturbed by the sounds; this nightly ritual has become somehow personal, threatening, as if dark fur and unknowable voices stirred in the room when the lights were extinguished.

She shivers a little with pleasure.

You can't, I murmur, go out now, and I feel her disappointment deep in me like bad meat, a sense that the soothing ministrations of the evening have not been enough, could never be enough in a world where there is infinite loneliness and men and parties. The soft blur of a strong drink. That's what she's after.

In my desperation, I become cruel. They don't like you here, I say. Remember when Sonia Italuk told the story about the Inuit princess who was so beautiful she made you look like a frog? She told it to make fun of you. The women say you think you're a movie star, the one on 'Dallas.' Remember, I prod. They don't like you, I say. You must be more circumspect. Flattery from men means nothing. You don't want to become a laughingstock. Small towns are cruel and kick you when you're down; remember home.

I can tell she is debating whether she cares. Her frustration pricks needles in my gut, and I am too full of pain to give her solace. We will not sleep tonight.

Tomorrow is Saturday and we can sleep in, I tell myself. And then it will be night and we will start the battle all over again.

But tonight there is yet a whole world to face, the world of night and the new spirits we are just getting used to. When we were children, familiar spirits sang in the fir trees and their songs were full of promises. In the newly revised edition of the world that claimed that girls could be anything they wanted to be, the spirits sang out to the small-town girls, telling them that if only they did not get pregnant, if only they could hold themselves in fresh innocent bunches like new flowers, they would find the deepest of loves and the most promising of careers. We waited. For what? For this?

The body is the temple of the Holy Spirit, she whispers to me, a low soft chuckle from the one I had hoped to put to sleep. It is the chuckle which draws men near, a vulval call, tempting, a call of hunger.

That's what you wanted, she says, more convincing now that she has unnerved me with the chuckle. You wanted the deep love and the deep thoughts. You wanted a briefcase and a suit. Not me. I only wanted to be touched. For me, the wind climbed under my skirt and made my thighs sing. But not in this godforsaken place. I have never wanted very much. You know that. It's hard to force a person against her inclinations. You must expect me to fight back.

Listen, I say, we'll get out of here in June. This place is getting to be too much for you. You need more stimulation; perhaps we both do. I am searching frantically for common ground. She recognizes the ploy. In the silence between us, the time from two to three a.m. seems endless. Only the sound of the wind, travelling across drifts, creating tessellations in the shapes of fish, winding around corners to make snow forts, huge crenellated battlements in front of our door; only the wind gives form to the formless night, the seamless fabric of insomniac time.

Half the people here don't sleep anyway, she states in a manner a little too matter of fact. I've seen them, she says, teasing. I leave your body while you sleep and I... she hesitates for effect.

...Go visiting, I finish, disgusted with such a cheap trick, with her amazing and galling conviction that she can tell me anything and I will eat it up like chocolate pudding.

...Yes, I visit. And I see them. And they're all like us, or a surprising number of them. Lying on their backs staring at the ceiling, listening to the wind. I've seen couples lying side by side, not even touching for warmth in cold houses where bodies should huddle together, staring at separate points of darkness, darker spots on a dark ceiling, the shapes of paint drips more absorbing than their lovers. There's a lot of people here that can't sleep.

Your grammar is becoming atrocious, I comment, and then finally I am ready for some levity. Look, I say, there are only about three hundred people in this town. You sure none of them sleep at night? Oh, Christ, we've got ourselves into a town of vampires. Nocturnals. The town plumber, played by Boris Karloff, is our only hope. Perhaps we can have a town meeting and reverse the order of things. Then you and I can sleep all day, I tease.

In the day we're not afraid, she says, then in a whisper— you're only afraid of the dark. Always were. The one safe thing and you're afraid of it.

IT'S four o'clock, she says, and I can still hear the guitar.

If I sleep now, she will have to. And as my insomnia is the edge that hones her desire, I am guilty. I can neither change nor satisfy, neither be still nor move. A new and different kind of stasis for me, stuck to a bed.

Remember the story, she says, that Marcella told about her aunt, the one who got tired of the world and went to bed forever. Her relatives had to tend on her for the thirty years she lived in bed, and she got a hump on her back from lying down. If I could sleep, she says, I'd go to bed forever maybe.

...Or if I had good company. She hums to the faint guitar carried on the wind. Know what they're singing? The St. John's Waltz.

I strain to listen but I don't have her hearing, her sharp senses. And I hear her catch the air of the song, run with it, send it back to the singers in the house two houses from ours where the teachers who a year or two ago were students in St. John's sing out in a drunken anthem their sentimentality, their desire to be back in the Thompson Student Centre rolling out chaotic choruses with little responsibility and just enough money for beer in their pockets. Instead they huddle in an unfamiliar landscape with the ballads of their pasts and hope they will learn the rules of this place so that they can stay without cracking up and perhaps even save some money.

We should go, she says, insistent this time. What's the point of lying here? This is just too shagging frustrating. Listen. They're having a good time. Nothing wrong with having a good time. Is there?

But I will not go. I have managed to keep us in until now and I am unwavering. No. You haven't been taking your pills lately. You'll go down there and, who knows, next thing you'll be sleeping with someone as lonely and desperate as yourself. Don't do this to yourself, I say.

I'm not desperate, she contradicts.

We can satisfy ourselves, I say, if that's what you want.

Now that, she answers, is desperate. That is the saddest thing in the world.

Since we were children, I have noticed a thing coming to a head in this shared life. I have seen her drop more and more away from the rules we have lived by; I have been watching the surfacing of a small, dark, glossy and careless animal, an otter perhaps, sliding to the water on a bobsled run of ice. So I turn and insulate, curled fetally, a small surrounding ball of comfort, until I can no longer stand the pain in my gut from her wriggling and struggling and her great private battle to be set free. At last I have to stand, defeated, and we walk to the window.

Outside during the interminable night, new battlements have been erected, our fortifications changed again, a new landscape each morning, independent unshakeable self-creations in a land where even a giant wouldn't bother to try to shovel itself out.

We watch wraiths in the wind that signal its changing direction, small curled sprites of a substance like icing sugar. The guitar is gone, either curled out to the frozen sea on the changing wind or else silenced by fatigue and drunkenness, no sound at all as the wind, as if pulled along on a harness, leaves the house down there and travels toward the harbour. In the trackless snow, the figure of Rudy Connolly, hapless academic and professional loner, negotiates the snow with the great care of the hopelessly drunk, each foot a choreographic statement, his head bent low in concentration.

Well, she says, indulgent, if he's a sample of who was at the party, you didn't have to worry about me. And she chuckles. Come on, let's go to bed.

So we try. It is okay now that the temptation of the guitar is gone. I feel her subside, and since I hold the ultimate keys to sleep, I try to sink with her, the only place I can, these days, follow her with any assurance of the outcome.

But I still find it difficult. I keep her safe for long spells with books and magazines, as many as I can lay hands on, with soothing herbal infusions ordered from health stores as far away as British Columbia, with the bath and beauty rituals played out with such ceremony. I am preserving her for a life somewhere else. I myself have no desire for these things, the pampering of skin and hair and soul; I am much too practical to spend money that way. But the sensual holds her for a while, as does music which must be listened to in privacy.

Still some folks here predict that if this windy cold continues and the snow does not gather on the high ground, the pipes will freeze and the water system will fail. I fear what will happen to her if she is deprived of the rituals for which water is a necessity. Will she use this as another justification for whatever she chooses to believe now? Will she tell me that now is the time to forget the pretensions of the life before? Going native—that's what they call it. An odd name since it is never natives who do it, but only the outsiders, dispossessed and displaced, whose lives are as breakable as eggshells.

Ssshhh, she says.

Ssshhh.

Stop worrying. It will be light in four hours.

Sleep.

December 12

*Last night I slept with Dave Marshall, and now I don't know what
to do. Annie knows—how can't she know with these thin walls? —
and she's walking around, not speaking to me, only stepping heavily,
shaking the floor when she moves around upstairs. It's been a
horrible day really, silent; I've got this feeling that everyone in town
knows. That's crazy.*

*I didn't really want to do it—it just happened. We were sitting
around, having a few after a nice dinner, and everyone left except
Dave. And then—things changed. They just changed somehow. I
hate the word "screwed" but that's how I think of it: that's what it
felt like, just "screwed." Now things will be awkward at school too.*

*We had the day off yesterday because of a particularly bad storm, and
a storm, like everything else, is an excuse for a party. I spent the day
looking out the window, feeling almost dizzy as the snow swirled
endlessly in eddies of wind. I felt as if the white powder was stealing
my breath even as I sat inside. The feeling of being trapped stayed
with me all day, so that even though I had the best of intentions for
the evening, by dark I would have spoken to anyone, joined any
party or cause or group or cult even, if such a thing were available.*

*Only occasionally throughout the day could any sound at all be
heard, any sound, that is, but the wind. Sometimes a skidoo would
pass by with a loud grinding noise as it pushed through the
deepening snow, occasional muffled lights through claustrophobic*

air, warnings on the local radio station not to go out. It was the sort of day when people said things like: "It was a day just like this one in '73 . . . right by his own doorstep." People here can always bring forth a memory of someone who had become so disoriented that he could recognize nothing but the terrible compulsion to sleep.

I can understand the compulsion, the spell of the snow. Like being sedated for an operation. So I stood in the window and watched nothing, and when dark came I craved company. We played cards until ten. Shot the shit. And everyone went home except Dave. Annie went over to check on Marian Carter to see if she's all right, and when she got back, she assumed I was asleep.

When I came in this morning, she looked up from the stove where she was cooking, and I instantly felt used, seen through, dissected. Dave's wall adjoins her wall. I thought I should go scrub this off, shower for a long time, but if I did, I'd be late for work. Annie was cooking bacon. She's usually chipper in the morning and offers me some of whatever she's cooking, mothers me almost, tells me I've got to eat more. This morning she stood and looked right through me, the spatula hanging in the air, dripping grease on the floor.

I didn't say anything. Only now I know I've broken some bond, some silent code that existed between us, and I don't even know what that code is.

I wish I could have slept in, gained some time in that private world of sleep to reconstruct my everyday self, to rationalize, to come up with a line of defence. Instead, I had to run off to work feeling raw and unprotected. Dave stayed out of the staff room, and Annie shot meaningful looks at me, as if to say, "Now, look what you've done." All in all a parcel of misery.

I feel like going back to the beginning of this and crossing out the words, as if that could make the event not happen. A childish ritual. Deny it. Lie through your teeth. Cross out the words. The whole incident is just another step towards loss of control.

The worst thing is that I don't even like Dave Marshall. He's a bigot and a chauvinist and, in any other place, he'd be the type I'd either ignore or bait with words, goad him to make him show his true colours. Here, I end up in his bed, wrapped around him, an erotic idiot. I will not deny that it felt good for awhile until I remembered who I was. Let's face it—we can all depersonalize in bed, become smooth moving parts, feats of fleshy engineering with not a thought in the world. Afterwards we sat and I smoked, and he gave me a look of disapproval. Then he felt guilty and tried to be tender, and that was the worst of all.

It would have been nice to get up and go home then, but I couldn't. It seemed worse to give up right away, as if doing so would be admitting just how shallow we were. We tried to talk, but we had nothing to say to each other. Most of the times when I talk to Dave anyway, he just rolls his eyes to heaven, and says something like, "Sheila, get a grip."

So we spent the night lying side by side, uncomfortable, unable to share space without poking each other with elbows or knees. Today we move about more separate and more isolated than before.

Did I say the worst thing is that I don't like him? Well, total honesty requires me to admit that the worst thing is that he doesn't like me and I know it. When he talks to women, he does it with a mixture of worship and condescension. We're all madonnas or whores to him, and he likes the categories. He's always been suspicious of me, as if he hasn't decided whether to place me on a pedestal up there or kick me into the gutter and spit on me. And now he knows I'm flesh and blood, and I feel that I have lost the tiny scrap of privacy I had.

When I went to work this morning, I kept my head down until I was safely inside my room. It's such a fishbowl, teaching. Even the kids look at you for some obvious humanity, and I know they watch me for signs of ordinary, human life. Did I give myself away, drop my guard at all? How vulnerable you are when you can't even tell if you're vulnerable.

I must try to write some letters, establish contact. The world is fading away out there; it's as unreal as the blue and green whirl of a spinning globe. And I'm running out of books. I must get someone to send me some books.

December 17

Pretty soon almost everyone will be gone except me. Holidays start on the 19th, and the next day there's a plane out. They're calling it the "evac flight." There's a lot of furious packing going on, and I feel a little mean, watching Annie packing up dresses with a fury as if she really has somewhere to go when she gets home.

Once when we were on the booze on a Friday night, she confided to me that she hates going home for Christmas. All her sisters are married and the whole family teases her about being an old maid. Annie has taught in a whole succession of these small communities, and every time she goes to a new one, her family wants to know the details about all the men there. In their eyes, her jobs are just opportunities to get married.

It's the kind of thing that really affects her, hurts her, because her job is so important to her, and yet I know that she wants what they have, except that she's broken too many rules to get it.

She'll have a New Year's night that will leave her wishing she'd never gone. Sitting with all the couples, listening to the inside jokes, a part and not a part all at the same time. All of the husbands will ask her to dance; one will allow his eyes to show he'd like to go further. It's such a predictable world, so smooth, the world we come from, the world of outports and bigger outports which try to call themselves towns, a world where you are either squarely inside or squarely out. No hovering allowed. I can tell by the look on Annie's face that she's setting herself up to be disappointed.

Not me.

I'm passing all this off as an experiment, how I want to get to know — really get to know — the local way of life. I want, I tell my colleagues, to get the sense of Christmas here, of how people celebrate the season, of what it's really like. I want, I tell them, to test my survival instincts, my ability to be alone. I've never been alone, I tell them; I want to try it. They look at me as if I've got an ulterior motive.

"You got more guts than I have. Either that or you're nuts. Staying all winter without going out! Take a break, girl!" Dave had said to me when we were still unencumbered and could speak to each other. Now he is sullen and withdrawn and convinced I'm nuts for sure. Especially after I cornered him and told him that I thought it would be best if we pretended that nothing had happened. He turned my own words back to me and said, "Why pretend? Nothing happened."

To tell the truth, I've always wanted to spend the Christmas season alone, without all of the messy connections that other people bring. At home, years ago: would Dad and Uncle Bud go out and get loaded and come home and get into an argument over who did the most work on grandfather's house? Would the women huddle in the darkness, curtains drawn, avoiding their "guests" who stayed all night half-passed-out sideways on kitchen chairs, their boggy boots making pools under the chairs for the women to clean up?

Women sitting in the dark, crunching humbugs, studying the flavour diagrams on chocolate boxes, watching the girl and the rainbow recede forever, crunching and rustling the only sounds except for the occasional whispered question as the latch clinked in the gate. They'd try to get the children's stuff together, hoping that none of the men would start singing shanties and wake up the kids.

Or at Derek's: should I give Aunt Letitia a present even though she hates me, and thinks her nephew has sullied his entire ancestry by 'consorting' with a Catholic? Such Christmases. Such parodies.

Every now and then, I pat myself on the back for my decision this year.

The school Christmas concert is tonight. I'm not having much to do with it; Annie's the kind of organizer who doesn't need much help. Essentially I'm responsible for keeping the Junior High bunch under control while little angels parade in a tinsel-strung pageant. I will help make sure the small shepherds go home with the right blankets, bathrobes and towels. I will think of how tender I used to feel about Christ when I thought of him as a baby.

I'm so bored today I could lie down and die.

December 21
Finally they're gone! The weather came down yesterday, and the plane couldn't get in. So last night we sat in the living room, a bunch of disgruntled teachers surrounded by mounds of luggage.

61

And we finished off the last of the tequila, and finally Annie came around and got out her accordion and we sang old Newfoundland songs until our voices slurred. Dave Marshall held out his jelly jar and sang, "Pour me another tequila, Sheila." I don't remember anything after that, and today I have a crashing hangover, like waves beating on a shore inside my head.

I was up at the airstrip with them this morning, seeing them off with as much cheer as I could muster, hugging a huge thermos of coffee against the cold. The morning broke with a high and cloudless sky, a brilliant sun that burns itself into your eyes and imprints violet spots on your vision if you don't wear tinted goggles. It was so cold at the airstrip that my forehead ached. And then the plane came in. I almost changed my mind and went with them; there was a spare seat and what, after all, of the things I use here did I really need to take with me?

For the first time in days, Annie really spoke to me. She looked concerned and hugged me before she left. Dave quipped with the boys about the "girls" who were waiting for him, then hurried toward the plane like God's gift to women going off to save all the lonely females in the world. I figure I've done something awful to that man; since he slept with me, he seems to spend all his time scurrying. He's gotten quieter. It's as if some of my introspection rubbed off on him when we were in bed.

After the plane had taken off, and I knew it was too late to change my mind, I went home and took the phone off the hook. I've been in bed ever since, and it's five o'clock now.

I rifled the rooms and managed to find a really bad novel to read, one in which international nuclear catastrophe is averted by the efforts of an intellectual with muscles to match his brainpower, and an ego to top both. He is aided, at first reluctantly, by a beautiful redhaired scientist who has never had an orgasm. Eventually, she falls in love with him and discovers both sexual and patriotic fulfilment.

Pulp is so wonderful, and, anyway, it's the only sort of thing I can find to read these days. I'd love to write a really good piece of pulp, but I've been told I'm too young to have the life experience to write anything useful yet. A piece of successful pulp would free me, though. I wouldn't have to worry about which outport I'll go to next year. Truth is, most teachers who go to these remote places consider it "doing time," building up experience before landing a job in a city or town. But I don't think that happens. Look at Annie — seven years, and she's no closer to even a small company town than when she started.

I've been trying to develop my poetry lately. But it's really pathetic. Every time I try to put something down on paper, I end up writing about the weather. Bloody weather!

I usually get stuck right at the first line, and I cannot even manage those sparse little snapshots I used to write at university. Nothing comes out except descriptions of the weather and bits of gossip. It seems that everything I write belongs in an almanac or scrapbook.

Oh well, it's sherry and consomme for me, half-and-half and heated, and back to bed I guess. I feel I could sleep for a week.

December 24

Christmas Eve. The tree is lit in the corner. Underneath, presents that came in the mail, still wrapped in brown packing paper. It looks like my Christmas presents are all mail-order sexual aids — I really should take off those plain brown wrappers. I'm drinking Grand Marnier, and there's a rhyme going through my head with a country and western twang in it:

I'm drinking too much

And I'm thinking too much

And the more I drink, the more I think

And the more I think, the more I drink.

Needs a chorus about being broken-hearted, doesn't it? Someone is still manning the local radio station, and through the static, Elvis's voice croons out at me, a special request from Vince to Elaine hoping she'll come back. I sing along, "I'll have a boo-hoo Christmas without you..."

December 25

So this is my Christmas entry, my "alone on Christmas Day for the first time in her life" sob story. But I don't feel like sobbing. I went to the MacLeans for Christmas dinner, and then we sat, stuffed, in the living room and drank whisky all afternoon. We listened to "Chestnuts Roasting on an Open Fire" in a sort of soporific stupor.

And I went to church where the grey and serious Mr. Graham could find, even at this time of the year, no joy in life with which to liven his service. The choir sang long, plaintive and melancholy songs which, stupefied as I was, I vaguely remembered as carols I had heard in another life. He preached about our blessings, the richness of our dinners, and the unfortunate truth that others in the world have never tasted giblet gravy. Then he passed around cards for pledges for a mission somewhere where the climate alone makes me want to travel.

I'm going to a party tonight so I'd better call home first. I must reassure the family that all is well before I continue sleepwalking through this holiday of mine. The oddest thing about today was opening presents alone. At least I didn't have to make appreciative comments about each one. I'd never thought of that before.

I remember the time that Derek gave me the silver slave ring — he thought it was kind of cute—and I rammed it on his little finger until it hurt. "Here, enslave yourself," I'd said, while Aunt Letitia almost fell out of her La-Z-boy in horror.

*I know well enough that I can get to feeling pretty sorry for myself,
yet this year everything being different doesn't make me feel that
way at all. I feel curiously afloat. Perhaps I've really been drinking
too much.*

December 26

*Some party! I was there for an hour when Gordon came in and sat
down by me and told me that Bernie and Ernie, otherwise known
affectionately as the 'Lockbuster Twins,' were planning a break-in.
They were loaded, he said, and they'd run out of supplies. "Gotta go
get us some emergency supplies, hey, boy," they'd said. "For sure,"
Gordon told me, "they'll hit up the teachers' residence. If I was you,
I'd go check it out. And take someone with you."*

*I was too angry by this time to take anyone with me, so I put on my
coat and boots and left without saying a word to anyone. This had
happened before; last time I lost a hundred dollars, and after that I'd
started stashing my money in dirty socks. Who would look in the
laundry for money? It worked, but I still lost a whole ham and six
bottles of wine on two separate occasions.*

*When I got home to the dark house, I was a little nervous. The boys
are not known to make graceful exits when caught. In the hall, my
breathing seemed hollow, and I could feel my heart pound. What the
hell do you think you're doing, I kept asking myself? Let them take
what they want. But something was riling me, firing up my anger
from the inside; it's that feeling of being violated again, having*

strangers poking through my things, being robbed by people who are convinced that I have no right to my possessions anyway.

But I had an idea, a sort of crazy idea. I knew that Rudy Connolly kept his shotgun in the porch next door. So I took the spare key and went and got it. Then I turned on only the lights on the poor lopsided Christmas tree that I had to put up to convince people that I'm not really from another planet. The gun wasn't loaded, of course.

So I crouched down behind the tree. The freezer's out in the porch, and that's the first thing the boys went for. Food. Then I hear, "What the fuck you want meat for, Ernie, get the liquor, they keeps it under the sink." So the door opens, and the first thing poor Ernie sees is a gun barrel pointed straight at him. "Jesus Christ," I heard him mutter, and he nearly took his brother with him as crashed out the door. I followed them out the door, and stood on the doorstep, brandishing the gun, and yelling after them, "That's right, run, run fast, or I'll blow your brains out."

Later as I sat on the floor picking up the contents of the freezer, I felt terrible, especially about what I'd yelled after them. It sounded like the right thing to yell. It seemed at the time that I could probably have done it. But what was my stupid act of bravado about anyway? It's like lately there are times I really want to do someone violence, to turn any act of violation around, to see it from the other side. Somehow I'm convinced that it would take away some of the resentment, that stupid hopeless resentment that builds and builds as I lose more and more control over things.

Anyway, the whole incident took the wind out of my sails.

Now I have to decide whether or not to report the incident. Nothing was taken, but the boys will be back. There's always a next time. And if I tell the police, then I'll have to say that I threatened them. That won't go over well; it's not supposed to be part of my role. Anyone can threaten me; it's a hazard of gender and occupation, and part of being an outsider. But I can threaten no one.

Let the matter slide? I don't know. The last time it happened, Constable Farrell told me that I could make up my own mind about whether to press charges or not. The boys, he said, went to jail every winter. Their house, he said, was cold, with an oil drum in the living room for a heater. They burned what they could find. They didn't have much there to make them stay. Nine of them under one roof, two cases of tuberculosis, a father with a persistent hack and a habit that required a lot of yeast in the brew bucket. They go to jail every winter, he'd said, to get out. They like it better out there in the winter. Then they come back in the summer and go fishing. Same thing every year. One of them had learned to read in jail. The grub, he'd said, was as good as in a hotel, free movies and visitors bringing magazines, chocolate bars and cigarettes.

I sat there listening to the picture he drew and, yes, I could see. But I was asking myself if this side of the story could be true, or was it just made up out of Brian's prejudices. Wanting to go to jail? It hardly seemed possible from my point of view.

If things are as bad as that for the boys, I should have a bit of sym-
pathy, have a heart. But I'm short on sympathy these days. I don't
care, my mind replies, too tired to assess any situation. I don't care,
don't care, don't care. I just want to sleep it all off.

It's Boxing Day. Appropriate name. I wake late at night and lie in
bed and listen to the sounds from outside. My mind feels emptied.
It's a night with a sky so high and clear you feel you're in a cathedral
and must worship. This clear air and far sky is something new to me,
air in which every sound is like crystal. I am used to a softer, muf-
fling sky, fog hushing voices and making the world seem smaller.

The voices of the dogs occasionally, long mournful cries.

And just now, a couple, walking home. They're starting the
argument now so that it'll be nice and hot by the time they reach
the house. I can tell he's tugging on her arm.

"Stop, for fuck's sake, stop it."

"C'mon, no lip from you, woman, you said enough tonight."

"Stop pulling me."

"I'll do what I like with you! You're goin' to get it when you get
home for fuckin' sure."

Listening to couples fighting on the road almost makes me homesick.
When we were kids, my brothers and sisters and I would crouch by
the window and watch fights on the road. My mother would try to

close her ears against the language; my father would get excited. We
all learned a vocabulary that would be useful later.

December 29

I got really depressed today. Seems I've lost time—how much?
Couldn't find any enthusiasm for anything, not even for food,
although the house is full of it. Finally, half-heartedly, I cooked up
some fish, then stared at it, stared around at the empty room and lost
my appetite. The trout on the plate got cold, the grease congealed and
its dead eyes were sizing me up. How could I eat something like that?

In the night everything echoes. Each sound is a ghost. Cabin fever.
When the others come back, they'll find a wild woman, crouched on
all fours, hair gone mad in a bushy halo. She'll look at them and not
recognize any of them.

I'm just writing this down for future evidence that I was conscious
today.

December 31

I'm getting ready to go to a New Year's Eve dance. I go to the
closet which is hardly ever touched, the one with my finery in it.
I open the door on the pathetic gathering, pick something in taffeta,
full, ruffled, red. When I put it on, my body slumps, feeling
unaccustomed to anything other than wool and corduroy. It is as
if nothing but the stiff, heavy fabric has been holding me up. I look
in the mirror, and the creature I see is neither fish nor fowl, an

uncomfortable hybrid. I look at my jeans folded on the bed and wish I didn't have to bother.

But tonight is an _event_. The women have been sending away for dresses for this since November, and arguing over who will order what when there's a tie for a favourite. The thing is that if two women show up in the same one, it might be murder. So I can't _not_ dress up; it would be liking putting down the party. But it's one of those nights when I cannot find myself, have no identity. I can always recognize this happening because, when it does, nothing I put on feels comfortable and, when I look into the mirror, I do not recognize myself. The reflection is that of someone else. Who is she, I ask, and I never can come up with an answer. So I put on different clothes, trying to be familiar to myself, wanting to recognize, to look suddenly and say, "There, there you are—that's you, girl." This dropping off of recognition is a thing that has happened to me before, only these days it seems more frequent.

Tonight, in the end, I chose the red dress, put on some jewellery, and then, of course, I had to put on a parka and skidoo boots with it. Quite the sight heading for the hall, remembering all the dances in my home town, the frenzied whirling, the smoke low and blue over the dance floor, nowhere to pee, and the inevitable fights that broke out once everyone was sufficiently worked up. This will be no different, I thought, and it wasn't. It's always a pattern. That was hours ago. I feel as if I've survived a seige.

Of course, there wasn't a bathroom. In the back, where the equipment for bingo and card games is stored, the organizers had placed a beef bucket for the convenience of the ladies. It was the sort of thing that required a pretty delicate and ungraceful balancing act, especially for those of us for whom high heels are curses, things alien to our slow, heavy-footed excursions over the snow.

There was a lot of laughing over the beef bucket, and some consternation when we realized that in all the preparations that had been made, just for us, no one had thought of bathroom tissue. We all had our little wads of tissues in our purses, but these would hardly last beyond three drinks. I was at the table with a glass of cheap bubbly in my hand when the solution came to me. "Cover your free," I said. "Didn't I see paper bingo cards in there?" And that was how the night went. Hoots, hollers, foolishness. Later, when the paper bingo cards were in short supply, we tore off the edges of the white and silver paper table cloths on our way to the improvised bathroom.

By ten-thirty, all speech including my own had slurred to the point where most conversations were hopelessly slow and often fragmented. I was starting to get bleary-eyed, tired, and sick of the whole thing. Sick of my separateness, the old thing, the unwanted childhood aptitude, to be there and not there, involved and not involved, that ability to float away and watch, to watch myself.

I imagined myself floating high in the corner of the room, looking down at myself dancing a wayward waltz with one of the community elders who had not given up yet on young women. From up there, I could see the look on my face, the look of surprise, of being out of place in a very definitive way. It was a very naked face despite the makeup.

I left the dance floor then and snuck out as unobtrusively as possible. In the back corner of the hall, a woman cried on a man's shoulder. I staggered a little, fumbling for my boots. I somehow wanted to get out of there before midnight, before the kissing and legitimized groping and the Auld Lang Syne.

I'm home now, sitting on the bed, rubbing my feet. I'm still in the garish dress, but I've wrapped a quilt around my shoulders. My feet are sore from the high-heeled shoes; it's as if my feet have widened, spread out in their big boots in the months I've been here. I'm being flattened, I think, coming to earth.

I'd have the radio on now, here in the dark, but there is no radio station at this hour, no contact along the empty airwaves to bring a countdown from far away. No St. John's Harbour. No Times Square. So I've got to get away to someplace else.

Happy New Year!

So this is the first entry of the new year and, since it is, should I try to make some type of New Year's resolution? But 'resolution' also means 'conclusion,' doesn't it, and I think a conclusion to anything in my tangled head is unlikely.

If I really wanted to make a resolution, I might start by promising myself no more disastrous parties like the one I left a little while ago, no more intrusions for me on other people's domestic unbliss. Tonight, I ended up a sitting duck, the object of a little scuffle between the keepers of a miserable marriage. So here's my New Year's resolution; I toast it with a solitary Scotch:

This time next year, I will contrive to spend the holiday really alone, somewhere in a quiet room with no expectation of anyone or anything, with no expectations of me. I won't go and get involved in things that are none of my business. And I won't drink.

Cheers!

Oh, this stuff is good. Cheers, again!

Somehow (how?) even this place seems to have enough people to intrude, to want things, things I can't give. I wish we could get radio here, but I'm dead tired now and feeling ready to wallow, and this is a time for wishing. I'm still wearing the foolish dress, and I curl up in it until no part of me is visible. Twice the phone rings, and I stay absolutely still, as if the caller on the other end can sense my presence if I move.

I know who it is anyway, so why bother. It's either the husband or the wife, calling to straighten things up or make them worse.

January 1, 10:00 a.m.

I used to swear that I'd never use this book to record events, use it like a diary, an almanac, an old mariner's observations of life at sea, the shifting weather. But this is something I have to write down. It may be momentous. I got up an hour ago, my mouth dry from last night, and I was badly in need of a shower. I turned on the tap, and all I got was a curious thin whistling that seemed to come from very far away. A brown drop of water then, forced out with the air. I've been phoning around, and it seems that the water has gone everywhere. System failure, that's what they call it. System failure!

I went to the kitchen and got the kettle and I've used what was in it yesterday. The worst thing is that last night I put on makeup, and now I can't get it off. Passionate Plum has turned to Putrid Plum, and now I look as if I've got two bruised eyelids. I suppose it will have to stay there until it wears off or winter melts into spring, whichever comes first.

In all the women's magazines I used to read once, there was a directive like a commandment: never go to bed without first removing your makeup. I used to think that it would just mean less than perfect skin, and having less than perfect skin anyway, I never took them seriously.

Now I know better.

Glamour knows about system failure.

Shit! Shit! Shit!

Happy New Year!

January 2

I am writing to put bitterness on a page. Perhaps it will self-destruct, the paper smeared with bitterness. Because for me the beginning of a new year has always been a chaotic big blow-out, a good time, and only after that do I get hit full-force with the introspection of January, that time when I have to sit inside because of the horrible weather and look out the window through the steam from the teapot and indulge in a sort of fierce self-interrogation about the past year and the one to come.

At retreats in high school, we would sit in the dark in the regional library and the nuns would ask, "Have you examined your conscience thoroughly? You must go deep, you must find every sin." And we would labour, digging tunnels into the depths of the subconscious until no sin remained hidden, or until someone farted, whichever came first. Some habits die hard.

In my self-imposed examinations during all these years when I've been feeling guilty about one thing or another, with dark January evenings coming down, I have looked at my mirror image growing in the window glass and, staring into my own eyes, asked, "So, tell me, what's going to be different this time? Are you going to smarten up?" and, when no answer presented itself, I would turn this way and that, to make my features distort in the glass, giving myself new features, widely spaced eyes and a chiselled chin. And now that the image returns to me I have to laugh, for I remember the careful choreography of that self-serving tragedy, how I looked and sighed and became every sad failed heroine I had ever read about.

In retrospect, I might even have dressed for these dreary occasions because, when the sessions ended, inevitably with an invitation to go somewhere, I was always ready to go out. Funny how these things stick out in the mind. That girl seems to me now a pretty silly creature, or perhaps I am a caricature of her, sharper, more pointed, more truly bitter. Let's say she's gone, and I don't know what to replace her with.

If I tried to do my January agonizing in the window now, my face would play back to me amid a raging storm, a dark face among a swirl of white powder, some conjured vision from a sort of snowy hell, a djinn right out of Sunday afternoon movies seen long ago on Film Carnival. So today I move away from the window and prop myself up on a pile of pillows on the bed. Like all other Januaries, however, I manage to feel terribly sorry for myself, except this time the feeling doesn't have the same sense of indulgence, but a harder edge I can't fathom and don't like at all.

And there isn't much hope of escape. If someone calls, it won't have the same effect and there will be no sense of a real change of mood.

On New Year's Eve I went to a party held down at the lonely end of town where there are only a few houses strung out along the shore. I made the point of getting there just before midnight—I couldn't be alone at midnight with the year turning over. I'd never been to that house before. The couple who invited me were keen on getting a big crowd. I went after I left the dance. They'd put a lot of effort into the party, with resurrected streamers from a previous year and a great deal of food and liquor. It always amazes me here, what people will do for the trappings of events. Not giving in to the land, to the isolation, the bitter cold outside; bright, extravagant things constantly appear which look like they should be somewhere else. And yet the else I remember never put on such a show of defiance.

I'd brought an almost full bottle of Drambuie and two bottles of cheap champagne which I'd barely gotten into before I felt I had to leave to keep the peace. It was a strange party, and all the singing and guitar playing was going on not far from the church where those who attended the New Year's Eve service greeted the year by remembering everyone who had died the year before.

Of course, it's good not to forget the dead, especially the recent dead. They may be, in more ways than one, still among us. Still, ringing out the old year by focusing on death always seems to me a little morbid. During the service, everyone is reminded that next year, who knows, they may be on the list, and everyone is sobered, figuratively and literally if needed, by such a prospect. So there they *were, thinking of the dead, and there we were, poised on the hill above them with our corks all ready to pop.*

The host was chugging my Drambuie and patting my knee all the time, holding out his beer glass of liquor to me and saying, "This is the good stuff, but you have to know how to drink it—this is the stuff you want to go down slowly, appreciate." Then he would proceed to chug down several ounces, pausing only to smile at me in deep satisfaction. All the time he kept patting my knee. I didn't know whether or not he was joking with me or if he really thought he was drinking slowly, but whatever it was, I must have been staring at him with quite a look of disbelief on my face, because his wife came over and sat down and, as soon as her husband turned to say a few words to someone else, she said, "Watch the way you're looking at my husband."

"What?" I said, not catching what she meant. Then, when I did, I said, "Oh, the liquor, oh that, I don't care if he drinks it all—that's what I brought it for, sure." And I know I was trying to sound very chipper.

But she looked at me again, harder this time, her eyebrows raised a little. "Don't try to play innocent. I saw the way you were looking at him."

And it hit me just a bit too late that she had mistaken my amazement at his chugging speed for the unbridled lust of a single woman with no place to dispose of her considerable libido. There's nothing like being a single woman in these situations! And before I could straighten her out, the wife had said, "Just watch yourself," and was gone out to the kitchen. Then this girl, Evie, a really shy girl, one of the silent ones from my evening upgrading class, came up to me and said, "Janie givin' you a hard time, Miss? She can get some crooked, I tell you. Once there was one of them student nurses here, and Janie's old man was goin' on the way he does, going on and on about her hair, you know, putting his fingers in it and everything, and Janie put a blasty bush in the fire and hit her over the head with it and her hair went all frizzy on top." I don't think I'd ever heard Evie say two words before, but she was obviously excited by the idea of a racket. Why is it that people love to watch women fighting?

It was about this time that the crowd in the kitchen started to count down . . . ten . . . nine, and I rose somewhat unsteadily because I'd drunk quite a bit and besides, I was now not only confused but a little scared that something unpleasant was going to happen between that woman and me, and in all my confusion, I pointed the champagne bottle straight at the light shade and a shower of glass rained down all over us. The injured wife was truly injured now, and when she turned around, there was glass sparkling in her hair like a bizarre decoration, and she told me she'd send me a bill for the shade.

Well, that was that. For the sake of saving face, I stayed to sing Auld Lang Syne and drink a glass of champagne with my hostess. I *vaguely remember trying to get on her good side, offering to give her the money for the shade right there and then. But I think she wanted to be pissed off for awhile. Then I did the safe thing and left.*

When I got to the main road, people were filing out of church, and several of them looked like they were crying or asleep, cradled as they were in the arms of relatives and friends. I sped past them, wondering if there might be somewhere else I might go (anywhere but home to the empty house), but feeling at the same time that I couldn't handle any more New Year's Eve parties. I sat on my skidoo by the harbour for awhile, looking at the flat whiteness where the sea should be, wanting to escape on its emptiness, but not quite drunk enough to commit such a foolhardy act.

So I went home to the dark house and this is the thing I hate — coming home from somewhere with my head full of spinning thoughts and my mind skidding around corners on two wheels. I like to either dance myself into exhaustion or get pleasantly blurry on food and drink. Either way, I can go to sleep easily. Instead, that night, I had to stay awake and think.

A roommate of mine at university once told me that when she wanted to sleep, she told her brain to shut up, turned off her thoughts and rolled over and went to sleep just like that. I have always envied her that skill, though at the time I wondered at the nature of a mind that obeyed such a command without questioning. My mind is disobedient. My mind has a life of its own and I have to doctor it, tranquillize it, as if it were a wild and probably dangerous animal. So after the curtailed party I poured myself a tumbler full of Scotch and went and sat on my bed and tried to make a New Year's resolution of some kind, so that the year could begin, if not with dancing, with at least one of the old safe rituals. But I couldn't come up with one; only the idea hinted itself to me that next year I should contrive to be alone somewhere, alone with my silly hopes for things turning out right and no nasty interruptions, calm days and nights, comfortable ghosts. And that night I wrote the foolish entry which I read today and shook my head over for its childish, Scotch-induced yearning.

The trouble is — I need someone to talk to.

The trouble is — in small places like this, we wear each other out too quickly.

And now today I sit here, having spent a day and a half alone, while the habits of my former life come creeping up on me, that staring out of the window until my head becomes a spinning chaos like the snow and I am in need of some type of rescue.

Rescue. On the crowded bus that took me over the dirt road to the high school where I spent my teenage years (mostly in the bathroom trying to avoid class; good training for a teacher), I would sit and dream about rescue, as the bus bumped and bucked beneath us. At thirteen, the rescue took the form of a predictable prince, one with all his teeth and thick glossy hair, and no discernible accent, one who rode horses instead of tying firecrackers to their tails. By the time I was fourteen, the rescue took the form of money, and at fifteen, it showed itself in the form of some daring opportunity, a risk I myself had to take. The rescue turned out to be no great adventure, but only a ride in a sweaty shore taxi with four suitcases bouncing in the back. I can't imagine a dramatic rescue now, only a long wait.

Yesterday was, I guess, a sort of typical Catholic punishment, and there's no punishment like the self-inflicted, and another practice in doing things alone. I'd had an invitation out for supper, but I said I'd stay home, "Naw, I'm cooking my own goose," I joked. It was really a very small chicken, and I'd already thawed it out anyway. Mustn't let food spoil. Waste not, want not.

So the window darkens, becomes a mirror. And this year I go for Scotch, not tea. I worry about the drinking, feel I'm getting caught up in something; sometimes a sour taste persists in my mouth all day. But tea heightens the senses and is well known for its diuretic effect. I need neither of these things, with my senses walking on a high wire and no water in the flush box.

And work resumes day after tomorrow. Tomorrow brings my colleagues, and these houses will be full again, full and empty at the same time. And with work comes January, month of introspection and returning light, the longest month of the year.

Jack The Trapper

Oona is the best hunter and trapper on the coast. For thirty years she has travelled the lines, following depressions and slopes, moving inland. Sometimes she takes one of her men with her, sometimes one of the older children, but it is her preference to leave them all behind, the children with Marta and the men to each other. When she comes back, nothing has changed but the stories. Now that Marta only goes to school— out of boredom—on Mondays and Fridays, Oona feels better about leaving the children anyways. When she goes into the woods, there is a leaving behind of all things; compactly, what she needs fits into what she and her machine can carry. Sometimes out there she runs into somebody else and offers them tea. Sometimes in return they offer her whisky. Not for work, she thinks, carrying whisky alone out there on the traplines.

These days there's a sad sight that she encounters out there from time to time, the man Carl, Carl F. Carter, that poor little specimen of a biologist who follows the land in a queer skittish zigzag like a rabbit—rabbit man. One day she asks him about his nervousness, has he always had it, but he only answers that he is just nervous around her, and then rabbits off sideways, up in the direction of Three Corner Bay where Jack the Trapper disappeared years ago.

Carl is one of the ones who brings whisky with him these days; perhaps he thinks that the men of the community expect it of another man. In case he meets anyone, he'll want to be hospitable. Perhaps he thinks that he'll be one of the men, and then it won't matter that his wife has left him and is spending her time with a man whose reputation with women is bettered only by his reputation at darts. Oona shakes her head after Carl's retreating back, sorry that the man knows too little to do the sensible thing and go home because dark is drawing in and he might encounter Jack himself sitting in the lee and having a boil-up.

CARL moves inland knowing it is too late to be doing this and not at all confident that he knows the trail. But that woman irks him, her sure confidence, her voice like the cold wind keening up to a crescendo as she tells him about the mad trapper and waits, teacup in hand, for him to suddenly change his mind about going further and decide to call it a day. Call it quits with his tail between his legs. Run away.

"Know what I think?" Marian had said, during one of their conversations in the long warm evenings before her flight. "Know what I think? I think that there are a lot of people here who're running away from things."

"Like what things, Marian? Who and what things?" Marian is aware of how important it is to him to be a scientist. Her irksome vagueness is something he wants to smooth out, and as soon as possible.

"Well, you know, like how a lot of the new world was settled. Pirates, thieves, criminals, broken hearts. That's who our ancestors were. There's no point in denying it. Who do you know who really wants to delve into their histories? Go really far back? It's because of all the skeletons."

"So?"

"Well, people need to do the same thing now sometimes, you know, can't cope or won't cope or loss of love or the pace of the city just gets to them. So they run away."

"And they come here?"

"Sure. Haven't you noticed, Carl, how many of the outsiders here would be outsiders anywhere?"

"No."

"Oh, come on! Just among the teachers and government workers and the like, I've met three people from recent break-ups and at least four alcoholics since I got here. Except I can't tell who are alcoholics anymore—everyone drinks so much. Oh yes, and a guy who thinks that gays should be sent to live alone on an island if not shot. What do you say to that?"

"Normal, Marian, perfectly normal, there are people like that everywhere. And much worse. It's just that we don't usually get to know them. A slice of life, this is," he finishes with a grin.

"Sometimes I think it's rubbing off on me. Sometimes I wonder if I'm not running away from something too. You know I was talking to Annie Peckham the other day and she was loaded or stoned or something, about eleven o'clock on a school night, and she was out of it—definitely *on* something. We were eating redberry pie up at her place. I kind of told her casually that I had trouble sleeping. The wind, and the silence. And she just took it as normal. Told me she hadn't slept for a month, until she got some pills from the nursing station. 'You should go down and get checked out,' she said, 'they'll give you something.' And I just nodded my head and smiled. And then she looked at me, meaningfully, and said, 'it's all free you know. All the drugs are free.' And I just smiled and thought, yes, maybe. A year ago, I would have thought it pretty strange. I would have thought she needed help."

"A year ago we were in Ontario," Carl says, his voice the verbal equivalent of a baleful stare. Carl is from Vancouver and he thinks Ontario is the stuffiest place on earth.

He turns to her, sees a genuine concern on her face. "You didn't get the sleeping pills, did you?" and watches her shake her head. "I love you," he says and goes to enfold her, red hair, eyes like green sparks, the smell of her sandalwood soap. It took him all his life to find her and he doesn't want her to move away now, apart from him, continental drift, although in some ways in their thinking they are, and have already been for awhile, worlds apart.

"Let's make love," he murmurs into her hair. She hates the way he announces things always, never daring to surprise her.

❀ ❀ ❀

OONA has an order to fill, thanks to the many requests for jackets from Etta, the best parka maker in town. Etta always uses Oona's furs when she can get them. They have been friends for a quarter of a century, and once they had shared the same lover. Only when he had died, drowned hunting seabirds, had each known about the other, and it had created a bond between them, a bond of memory and empathy that time only strengthened.

Fur for the hoods, for some, those who made orders from the city, fur even for the cuffs and all the way down the front. Oona is careful not to snicker in front of anyone who she thinks might have ordered one of these. Only she thinks that fox on jacket cuffs is pretty impractical, must only be for people who do not work. How else to avoid grease and blood and oil on them? Oona does not cluck her tongue because this is cash, and she could just as well convince them that they needed fox rears to sit on to pad their delicate kidneys. Money in the pocket, she thinks, and the more the better because she has just found out that Marta is pregnant and the father of her child has disappeared with the boats, gone with a full load of shrimp. Marta will be no good for plant work this summer. Or for fishing or even the smoke house. Oona rolls a cigarette and smiles at the idea of being a grandmother. In good time, she thinks, I'm forty-two. Marta is sixteen. Not like me, Oona thinks, who started so late.

CARL has always been thin but there is something about the woman Oona that makes him feel like a dwarf whenever he meets her. Now, encountering her on the trail, large as life and on snowshoes, he watches as she uses the encounter to stop and roll a cigarette, light up, surveying her surroundings all the time, and finally, "How's it goin'?"

"Fine, fine," Carl says, pissed off at himself for repeating the word, but not knowing how to respond to this question, as general as the horizon, that he had first encountered in the outports of Newfoundland and, now, here.

"Well," Oona smiles, pointing her cigarette for emphasis, "You're the only man I run into out here who comes and goes without taking anything with him. That's good," she grins, "you're not my competition."

"I make notes," he says feebly, "on migrations." There is a temptation in him to use lengthy words she will not understand, the kind of words that put off further questions, although it seems to him that her command of two languages is excellent, and the effect would probably be lost. She is not easily disconcerted. He does not wish to hate her, but standing in front of her he feels that he is taking an exam and is failing. At night sometimes he has dreams about the oral defence of his dissertation, and in these dreams it is Oona who questions him. Perhaps it is just that he is so small and Oona is so big; perhaps, after all, it is as simple as that.

* * *

AT night, after an astonishing dream in which Carl stands before an assembly of hunters and trappers to defend his dissertation, and Oona is the chief inquisitor, Carl wakes with his throat constricted and Marian does not notice his agitation but continues, at first, to stare at the ceiling and it appears that she has been doing this for quite some time, lost somewhere.

"I've got to get out of here," she breathes. "If only for a while. Carl?"

"Yes?"

"It's different for me. You have your work. You have a sense of purpose, you spend your days doing something you want. I hate substitute teaching. I hate even worse those days when there's nothing to do except go to someone's house and watch the damn soap operas. I don't mean go away forever. Only for a while."

"I wish you didn't do that..." Carl says as she reaches for a cigarette. "You never used to."

"Call it a crutch, if you like. I need it. I need more of them, to tell the truth." There is a bitterness in her voice, gone the tenderness that drew him to her like an unfurled ribbon. In the beginning, she had reminded him of what his mother used to say about a cousin of hers who had died young, existing now only in the frame of a photograph, an angel with floating hair and liquid eyes. "She was too fine for this world..." The expression had come to mind when he'd seen Marian on campus, and she seemed to him so rare and fleeting that he had wanted to be the bond that held her to the mortal world. If he looked hard, underneath the tired eyes, behind the cloud of cigarette smoke that gave her voice a rasping quality, perhaps he could still find it. Perhaps if he helped her to leave he could keep her as she was. And when his work was done...

"Marian," he says finally, giving her the very tenderness that could make her stay, not lecturing for once but only giving her the best of himself. "If you want to go for awhile, I'll give you the money for it. Go for a vacation. You can come back when you want. Or I'll meet you this summer back home."

Marian has not anticipated this gift of freedom. She leans into his shoulder, but he will not love her now. For Carl there is love and there is separation, no blending of the two, no other place. Having freed her, he has tangibly let her go. It takes her six days to leave the house. But the weather comes down and she cannot leave town. She looks for a place to stay and wait.

❋ ❋ ❋

"YOU'RE not careful, you'll end up like old Jack the Trapper," Oona tells Carl in the shade of a tuck with cups of tea against a sudden upsurge of wind like needles.

"What happened to him?" Carl asks, not really interested.

"Don't know really," she says. "He lost his fight. He lost his spirit."

Carl walks home on snow that crunches in its brittle freeze as if the ground underneath has somehow gone hollow, as if the

earth is really elsewhere, as if one had landed somewhere where
the trusted consistency and solidity of the earth had no
relevance. This crunch, this echo of disbelief, could drive you
crazy if you thought, even for a moment: this alone exists—a
hollow earth—a shell of ice.

Ride over it and another thing happens; the hollowness is
displaced by the comfort of noise and, no matter how hard you
ride, how heavy the burden you carry, it will not give away.
Instead the constant pressure of machine-driven skis makes
deep depressions, corrugates, a thousand deep ridges. In the
afternoons, the sun gathers a hard gold in these depressions;
deeps and highs are defined containers of gold, as if there is
after all both depth and richness in the landscape. To ride over
it is to choose speed and sound, the noise of mechanization,
over the insecurity of your own footsteps.

Carl hears the echo, a grinding sound that reverberates
through the body, sees the pools of trapped sunlight. January.
He had expected misery to yield a landscape white and flat,
faceless, an easy one to leave; instead it has delivered up this
clarity.

Along the airstrip, markers made from snow stand like
cones along the sides, marking the way for the planes to land,
the planes somehow made playful by that instruction to veer in
between the cones, so many constructions of a child's whimsy
showing the way to avoid accident. From each cone of snow an
evergreen branch protrudes, like Noah's green branch, Marian
had said, a token of the security of the land. No red triangles
blowing in the wind, no arrows or red-amber-green dictates of
the busy airports of the outside, no lights. Only the evergreen
branches in the uptilted mouths of the doves of snow.

Coming in in the afternoon light, the surrounding moun-
tains fill up with light just like the ruts worn in the snow. The
valleys of colour in the midst of the black rock had reminded
Carl, on that first visit, of liquor or stained glass. There is the
pale gold, the colour of champagne seen through a chilled glass.
An iced blue that only the eyes of ice dwellers know well

enough to describe, a translucent grey that is like the edges of fur when the light comes through it at the end of a hood.

Flying up the coast on someone else's charter, he had seen colours that he had not seen before, and he had tried to write and tell her about it because there was in him an instantaneous desire to invite her to come and live here with him, so that he could live long enough among the colours to find names for them. He had that feeling that the uninitiated sometimes get that if he could live long enough among such colours, amid such landscape, his life would be immeasurably enriched, as if he had experienced something deeply spiritual, knowledge that the rest of the world had no access to, secrets that would give him an edge, what kind he did not know, but an access definitely. For Carl, coming here had been as much about the sense of a privileged view of things as it had been about the private habits of migratory animals.

Then when he had tried to write Marian about it, to persuade her that it was worth the trip just to see the colours in the hills, tried to describe the infinite range from white to blue as he had seen it, like being inside an iceberg, his language had failed him. He didn't know the words. He had only been able to tell her about how the ice ended and the dark blue sea with its unknown inhabitants had begun. He had ended up writing the feeble words of a typical proposal, and he had feared failure. Instead she had accepted without question. She had called it a leap of faith.

❁ ❁ ❁

"HE was a white man from England who tried to be an Inuk." Oona tells him another time. "Was running away from something, for sure, the old people said. Came here when I was a little girl. Lived wild, he did. Alone. And always in a hurry. Look," she says, stretching her hand out to enclose the whole of the white open world, the off-white of sky and bay all blended together into a world with no horizon, "where is there to hurry here?"

92

Oona is drinking today, uncharacteristically, knowing that drink creates a deceptive warmth which convinces you to lie down and sleep. Only today it's warmer, a low front turning everything the same indistinguishable hue, making the air touching her cheeks a pleasant minus fourteen. No danger drinking unless the weather comes down bad. Her husband has come back. Last night he showed up just like that with presents for Marta and her baby, a sentimental man, crying into his beer late at night so that Oona was ashamed of him in front of her children. He had thrown her men out of the house, as if he had any rights. Oona had had to leave. If I leave, she'd thought, he'll leave. He's only in town anyways for a drunk with his old buddies and then he'll be gone. Oona had fought him once, tooth and nail, fought him with her entire body, and she had grown tired of it. She has no desire in her body anymore to fight with men. She is too busy. She has what she needs.

"My husband came back last night," she says, "to pick a fight. He does that every now and again—gets sick of bawlin' out his new wife and kids. Came back because we're going to be grandparents. Tears in his eyes, and everything."

Carl doesn't know what to say. He tries to imagine Oona having dimensions other than the ones he has given her. It is strange. And he does not want to know all about her, as burdened by stories as he is. Oona smiles through the steam of the boiling kettle and waits for his response, but Carl is digging deep inside his knapsack, coming up eventually with a tin of ham, a loaf of bread and a tub of margarine. He places them in front of her, a tea offering.

"So," he says at last, "Tell me what happened to old Jack."

"John Furness was his name. There was talk," Oona says, "that he killed his wife. Back in England, that was. Anyway his wife disappeared some time before he came over here. He used to be a minister. Sometimes when he got loaded he would stand in the snow and take his clothes off and pray to God to forgive him, although no one knew what he wanted God to forgive him for. You can imagine a lot of people listened pretty close; they wanted to find out, see, if he really killed his wife. But he never said. Mostly stuff from the Bible. Some of the men used to say that really his wife left him for another man and he went crazy. Anyway, he fell in love with a young girl here and she wouldn't have nothing to do with him because he was so old, and he couldn't stand it. That was when he began to spend all his time alone. All the time alone. Gone for weeks at a time. Lived on what he caught. Then he would come to town, sell his furs, get drunk, and preach another sermon from a snowbank. In the morning then, he'd be gone.

"One time he left and didn't come back at all. We wondered, like you would, what happened. But he was a strange man. Then there were stories, stories that people had seen him moving over the snow at a great speed, down on all fours like the animals he was hunting. And then my David, the young fellow who drowned, he came back one day and said he'd seen him. Jack the Trapper was on his knees and frozen to the ground. David said he'd never forget the look on his face, the queerest look he'd ever seen on the face of a man. Fear, like, but something different. And no marks on the body. David came back in a hurry to get men to go for the body. And when they got there there was no body. Only marks in the snow like something got dragged. But no blood or fur or signs. Just the marks. Nobody could account for them marks. And, well then, no one believed what David said. That broke him up a lot inside, you know. Like he was crazy or something, seeing things. But the next fall David was drowned himself out hunting for birds. No one ever for sure found out what happened to Jack, you see, because he was gone, that was all, and nobody ever came from England or anywhere to ask about him. Maybe he's still out there somewhere. Perhaps my David saw a wolf and his nerves were playing on him and he thought it was Jack. Anyway, he's a good one for frightening the kids with when you don't want them straying too far."

"Well, I don't know. You tried to frighten me with him. And I'm no kid."

"No," Oona says, sizing him up, "No, I s'pose not."

94

* * *

ON a windy day, the kind that bends you in half and makes
outdoor work impossible, Carl goes to see Marian where she's
babysitting for the afternoon and tells her about John Furness.
He wants to amuse her, for her eyes are ringed with dark, flabby
circles and her breath is bad as if she's been eating and smoking
and drinking all the wrong things. He brings her a fish. He
wants to make her laugh but senses only tragedy in her face. At
last when it is time for him to go and she has not laughed, he
asks her if she has her ticket in case the plane comes soon. She'd
slept in and missed the last one, the first in a few days, and he
couldn't account at all for her lethargy, the way she moved as if
suspended in a slow dream, the way she seemed to have lost
control of herself.

"I don't have all the money," she says wearily. "I spent some
of it."

There is no need to ask her out of what necessity the money
has been spent. Moreover, it seems callous. Tonight he does not
lecture her, but she senses that he wants to, that his finger is
dying to point. That he has in him enough prepared speeches to
last a lifetime. But he's tucked the offensive finger in his pocket,
and now he takes it out, folded with the rest of the hand around
a wad of money. He presses the money from his hand to hers,
and for a minute she remembers handholding in a park on a
Sunday afternoon, as if the picture comes from the memory of
another incarnation of herself, a snapshot from a more innocent
time, perhaps the turn of the century.

"Please go soon," he says urgently. "Please leave as soon as
you can."

January 6

*What a hullabaloo when the bunch came back and discovered the
water situation; it was as if they'd never been here before, and were
total newborns to the situation. Or tourists wishing they'd stayed
home. They went around turning on all the taps, listening to the
empty whistling in the water lines, as if I'd told them a lie, just to
shock them the minute they arrived on the doorstep. Like — ha, ha,
guess what, we've got no water.*

*I told them that I had the situation under control; it was very simple.
First you take a large oil drum and light a fire, letting it burn until
no residue is left. Then you lash the cleaned drum to your komatik,
hitch the komatik to the skidoo, take a small bucket with you, and
drive up to the stream on the lee side of Three Corner Bay. There you
dip out the water in the small bucket and transfer it to the drum.
Thirty-seven buckets — I've counted — and the drum is full. You
have to put snow on top of the water to keep it from sloshing out. The
first time I went, I didn't know about the snow and the water
sloshed, every time I hit a bump, down the back of my neck.*

*It was twenty-six below that day, and I felt that I would have
pneumonia. When I got back to the house, the water had to be
unloaded with the small bucket again, into more buckets on the
kitchen floor. By that time, pneumonia had begun to have a certain
attraction, and as I carried bucket after bucket, I thought of myself
recuperating somewhere, a private rest home in a warm climate,
me in a white lawn nightgown hopelessly confined to my bed,*

languishing amid floral gifts, like Bette Davis in an old movie,
somebody bringing a nourishing breakfast which I can't — simply
can't — eat — no, don't try to press me — my appetite is like a
bird's.

But that is merely another version of the fantasy of rescue. By the
look of things, I'll be spending my evenings this winter carrying
water from bucket to drum to bucket, and still never get enough to
take a bath.

Of course there had to be a party to celebrate the teachers' return.
They were well stocked up for it too. Boxes were unloaded, and
spices, condiments, taco shells, cheeses, smoked meats, olives,
pastries, vegetables and fruit poured out. And liquor of course. There
was a big fuss about giving poor Sheila a treat, and dinner followed
with everyone wearing the new clothes they bought on holiday. Their
pants were creaking and their sweaters had store-creases in the
sleeves; they reminded me, with their new haircuts, of kids at the
beginning of the school year. Sometimes I feel as if I am watching a
movie, that we are other people somewhere else, the British in India
perhaps. Rescue, salvation come so easy, poured out of big cardboard
boxes, things from the city. I listened to the stories, but everything
seemed unfunny and irrelevant. The way they talk you'd think St.
John's is the end of the world, the cradle of civilization.

But I enjoyed the food. And Annie, in her organized way, made up a
schedule for us, the water-bearers, to follow. I've only got to carry
water three times a week. It's no use scheduling anyway — people

here are kind, and I know some of the men will bring water when they can.

Dave has shaved his beard, and now looks younger and even more unattractive than he usually does. His chin seems to float in front of him. Last night, he called me aside and said he'd been thinking of 'us' over Christmas, that he thought we might be able to have a chance at a relationship, if I was game. It was very sad, really, him trying to do what he understands to be "the decent thing," and me thinking about no longer being alone and a curiosity, prey to straying husbands.

It would be so easy, I thought, as I sat there watching him. What could be more natural, two young single teachers with few parts missing, finding romance on the coast. Keeping each other warm. And I thought of how sad and desperate I felt the morning I woke up with him. It simply wouldn't work. So I shook my head and looked out the window at the northern lights and avoided his eyes. He left then. I hope that things can get back to normal, whatever normal is.

The thing that really bothers me about the water being gone is that I can't seem to get clean. I've always been fanatical about long baths. Now I've got to do sponge baths in the sink, leave my hair for days until I can smell it, oil and lanolin; I remind myself of the sheep we used to keep when I was a child. Then there is the thing about shaving my legs, a habit which I wish I could give up, but I can't. It's one of those things that has been drilled into me. Now I put one leg up on the sink, a sort of balancing act, and leave the other one to

99

anchor me to the floor. And all the while I wonder why I bother. But this little ritual seems important. I feel sometimes that my contact with who I am, and who I have been, is tenuous at best. I feel that with each habit I might change, each meaningless ritual I might relinquish for the sake of convenience and comfort, I would come to recognize myself less and less. I might not be able to live anywhere else then.

There's a little new blood here now — a woman named Peggy O'Leary arrived on the plane with the teachers. She's the new social worker or, as people refer to her here, "the welfare." I haven't met the welfare yet but I intend to. Perhaps she will be a contact, a point of sanity; perhaps she will look around at the absence of water and vegetables, the children sick or pregnant or bored with life, the silence that surrounds us and not dismiss it as 'normal.' Perhaps she will complain, and refuse to take everything in stride. I get so sick of taking everything in stride.

It would be refreshing to find someone who finds certain things unsatisfactory. I come from a place where people complain about everything, all the while protesting that they don't. But here I'm not allowed to complain; I have it too good. You're only allowed to complain if your family's been here for three generations. The other day in the store I made a mistake of commenting to the cashier that it was hard with the water gone. An old woman in line behind me then took this as an opening, and recited a litany of all she had to do in her day. "And we had dogs to feed," she concluded, making no bones about the fact that she thought young ones like me wimps or something worse.

It's the same thing at school. I can't let on that I find anything less than it should be. It's like an insult, a statement from an outsider that 'puts the place down,' and that is not my intention. I wish only to have water, carrots I don't have to shave the hair off, an occasional orange. I'd like someone to patch that crack in the window made by a stray snowball. But I have to be careful not to sound like a colonizer.

It's a funny thing, this whole notion of colonization. As if I could be a colonizer—me from an outport, fisherman's daughter, inheritor of poverty and hard knocks. But most of the people here do not make that distinction, that being from the outside does not necessarily mean privilege, only difference perhaps. And my students refer to me as 'lucky.' "It's different for you," the older ones say, "You're lucky, you are—you have an education. And you're making lots of money." It's as if an education, like a birthmark, is something you have no control over. And since I'm lucky, I have no right to complain.

It means that people have access and certain rights to me. To my privacy. To what I think. Sometimes it's like having a bedroom with no door, all eyes peering in. Seasoned teachers tell me, get used to it, girl, it's the same thing everywhere.

All the same, some times I do feel like a damn parasite, making money off those kids.

January 9

Last night I dreamed about Derek for the first time in several months. In the dream I am walking by Quidi Vidi Lake, and I stop at the edge of the water to skim pebbles on its still surface. In the water, I see a shape define itself, moving toward shore. As he comes closer, I can see that he has been drowned for some time; his body is bloated, lifeless. Yet he advances toward me, propelled by something more than the slow currents of the lake. On the margin of the shore, he raises his head, opens his mouth. Out pours a cascade of water and some small fish, pricklers maybe. "You know, Sheila," he says sadly, "I'll never get out of here alive." And I know that he is already dead, but don't have the heart to tell him.

When I woke up with my heart pounding so loud that I could actually hear it, I felt not only terror but a great sense of loss. It was as if I realized for the first time how great a change I had made for both of us when I broke off the engagement. I had lost a lifestyle, and so many familiar things, and I wondered if he felt the same. And instead of mourning the loss, adjusting, I had come here, to a routine of work and lonely nights and excessive drinking, a situation tailor-made for anyone with a tendency to self-destruct.

I've been sitting here thinking about that, and I can't sleep. Right now, I feel like going to the cupboard and taking out one of my hoarded bottles. Because liquor is the only thing that makes me sleep, the only thing that lulls me and takes the sharp edges off my thoughts. Preventive medicine to keep me from being a zombie tomorrow. A placebo to allow productive days, nights that pass in the blur of a shifting dream. I am restraining myself.

In the next room I hear muted sounds, sounds of bedsprings moving in a sort of slow and desperate monotony. Marian Carter has come to stay in the spare room; she looked so pinched and disoriented when she showed up that we could not refuse her. It seems that she's had some sort of break with her husband, Carl, and she's planning to leave. When, I don't know. And now she's taken up with this guy Jack Barker, descendant of the original colonizer, I'm told, and the other day she was talking in a very cheerful and almost dreamlike way of maybe settling down here.

I wince when I hear her talk. And I know that she doesn't have what it takes to put up with Jack in the long run. He's being very nice to her now, courting her, treating her like a piece of exotica, but that will end. You can tell by looking at him that he is the sort of man for whom the chase is the ultimate, and that it gives him particular pleasure to steal a woman away from "that frigging little biologist," Carl. Carl over in the experimental dome house with his papers and books, the postcard outsider.

I can see why she found it difficult there; that house alone separated her from everyone around her, made her, by definition, suspect. And Carl was always gone. She told me that the day she decided to leave, the wind had been high and was moaning around the walls. In the kitchen where she tried to work, the pots and pans rattled on their hooks. She had felt that the walls, the kitchen, the clanking utensils were about to lift away and up, leaving her stranded, her hands held high. The rattling had gone inside her head. She had wanted to be anywhere else, just to be around people. She has told me a few other things about her life, but mostly she remains a mystery. One thing that I know, though, is that she's not as fragile as Carl thinks. It's too bad she had to find this way to prove it. Carl put her on a pedestal and, poor girl, she fell off.

Now she's in there with Jack, and I feel the heaving of the bed as it bangs the wall behind my head. Sleep would be a mercy. These thin pre-fab walls tell too much, much more about Marian than I want to know.

I will recite to myself — sleep, sleep, sleep — like a mantra until I can. And pray the Lord my soul to keep.

January 17

I have been asked if I want to go out to a conference on Social Studies. "Yes, yes," I said, and then I went to the washroom and grinned at myself in the mirror — what a social study I make myself! Since we lost the water, I can't seem to keep my hair clean, so I have taken to pinning it back and up. It hasn't been cut in a while, so it keeps spilling over hair bands and pins. My skin has gotten really dry from the cold, and there are red sore-looking patches under my eyes. I've really let myself go. I'm down to the last of my clean clothes, so I've been wearing this unflattering baggy blue sweater for three days. It looks like a recycled baby's blanket. My lips look like old linoleum.

I can just see me around a conference table, biting my nails, sizing up the men.

Perhaps I will burn up on re-entry.

January 22

We have now had twenty days of sunshine. Straight. No clouds, except some high wispy ones like angel hair, barely there at all. Down through the blue through the crystal air to the white snow, a blazing sun pours, its heat felt directly for a moment on my shoulder though the rest of my body is freezing cold.

Sometimes when I look at that sky, I can imagine heaven. Childhood heaven from a book of juvenile prayers.

Sometimes the landscape is so beautiful here, it's too beautiful to take.

I am watching my students run around outside at recess. In this landscape, their legs lift so high above the snow that they look like they are dancing on a white moon. They are so much a part of it that they don't notice what makes them so exuberant.

Blues, whites, greens, crystallines. These are the exact colours of the tropics, only frozen.

January 24

I made a point of going to visit Peggy O'Leary. She's different. Definitely.

I just re-read my last entry. The tropics! I've never been to the tropics. I must be nuts.

Certainly, my dreams are nuts. I dream of fruit. I dream of fog. I long for both. You could probably get locked up for wishing for fog.

January 31

Peggy O'Leary has glass bottles of spices around her kitchen walls. She has ginseng in a jar. When the sun shines in through her windows, it lights the spice bottles, and the words on the labels seem like the words of incantations or magic cures. Cumin, thyme, sage, coriander! Lemon grass, cinnamon, dill weed, ginger!

Last night when I was there, she melted chocolate, dipped tinned pears in it, and served it up with Amaretto-flavoured coffee. I was stunned. There is something about the way she does things — slowly, carefully—that makes ordinary things seem important, ritualistic, and if you're there, it makes the occasion seem special.

Peggy was born in Toronto, but her parents are from Newfoundland. She came back to Newfoundland to go to university because her parents thought it would be cheaper, and she stayed. She says that she wants to see beyond buildings to the true landscape, and she couldn't do that in Toronto. "You'll have no problem seeing the true landscape here. It's everywhere." I said.

"Yes," she said, "The houses seem almost incidental. The landscape is almost too much."

I know that I'm getting paranoid, because even though I don't think she actually said it, what I heard was "too much for you." Could she see that I have trouble sleeping? Trouble teaching? Trouble coping? I felt it.

We had our pears and coffee, and she invited me to come again. Anytime, she said. And she asked me about Marian Carter. She just said she'd like to meet her, but again it seemed that there was more said, that she knew all about Marian. Maybe she heard that Marian went on a crying jag in the store last Thursday. Several people saw her there crying and holding up a bag of moldy onions, saying again and again, "There's no need for this, there's just no need." It didn't take the story long to get around. I told Peggy that I'd tell Marian how good the food was, and maybe she'd better go and try it. Peggy laughed at that.

When I got home, Marian was standing in the porch, saying goodnight to Jack. I could tell by the low growls of their voices that they'd been arguing about something. Marian was standing there in a long flannel nightgown with violets on it, and her bare feet in the slush of the porch were turning the same colour. When she came in and sat down, she turned on the TV and just stared at it.

"I was just up to Peggy O'Leary's," I said. "We had chocolate-dipped pears. She asked about you."

"About me? She doesn't even know me."

"She just said she wanted to get to know everyone."

"Yeah, right!"

Marian is starting to sound like Jack. She just sort of snorts when you talk to her, bites off her words and spits them out. Maybe she really has to have a man all the time. And maybe she takes on their attitudes, or they rub off on her or something. First she was sort of like Carl. Now she's more like Jack.

Two weeks to conference time!

Beast in the Dark

ANNIE PECKHAM is a practical person. Nobody would ever dispute it. Her parents think that maybe she's a little too matter-of-fact, or she'd be married already. If you want to find someone to marry, you can't be too practical.

Annie is holding her parents' latest letter in her hands. Her mother's words are full of details, full of loving descriptions of her grandchildren. She has been knitting for them all, baking for them all. Then at the end of the letter, her father's few words, full of the old tease, and ending with, "Your mother doesn't have the nerve to ask you, but have you met anyone?"

Annie turns off the light and lies in the dark with the letter warm and wrinkled in her hands. She could tell them that after the absoluteness of their love, nobody has ever made her feel warm and welcome. She puts the letter under her pillow, and closes her eyes. And waits. Today, since dark, she has felt at the back of her throat the familiar catch of a threatening presence. Too indefinite to be shrugged off as a cold. So she waits.

And sure enough, it comes.

The first indication of its presence: the dark becomes darker. Some greater blackness swells inside the dark and fills it up, until she can make out a heavy shape, a thickness. The shape moves, rearranges itself; its outlines are forever shifting as it flows toward the bed.

And then it's there. Right there.

No, she wills it, go away. Attack someone else.

Annie feels the thing climb onto the bed, exerting a great effort to pull itself along without legs, without arms. It oozes over her feet, her legs, laying cold and numbness there, up to her groin, stomach, until finally it settles on her chest, spreading itself, its face pushing against her face. By the time it has nestled here where her body breathes, pumps blood, the chill numbness has become something else: terror.

Then it is as if all the air is being sucked out of her. She feels the iciness settle in her feet and hands, the numbness complete itself through her arms and legs, a tingling that ends in no feeling at all. Under the blankets, she touches one hand with the other for reassurance. But what she feels doesn't seem to be part of her body at all. It could be marble or stone, steel or concrete, just a solid object, no more a part of her than the thing lying on her chest. The things breathes, and when it does, it is with Annie's own breath. "Get off me," she whispers, "Get off!"

She can't breathe at all. Her heart hammers inside her, loud enough for the whole house to hear. Surely, someone must hear her heart pounding. Marian! Sheila! Someone will hear and come, knock on the door and ask if she is all right. And the thing will be frightened, as it always is in the presence of others, will slide off her in a hurry, and ooze out through the crack in the window sill where the wind enters.

Nobody comes, and Annie waits for the moment of unconsciousness.

I'm dying, Christ, I'm going to die. Panic. A long and empty space where the thing sucks the air out of her body. Paralysis.

At the moment when death should come, and is almost wished for, the beast always lifts its muzzle away from her face, just a little, and she feels the rush of free air and gasps for it. Slowly, slowly, the beast begins to lift its heavy body and slide away. Annie knows this moment well, and she clocks the changes and returning sensations. First, the awful constriction in her chest gives way, then her jack-hammer heart begins to slow. A creeping sensation of warmth tracks its way through her limbs, moving from centre to extremities until finally she can feel fingers and toes again. It is a long time before her feet

110

regain feeling, a seeming eternity before she knows she could walk if she wanted to.

She rubs her feet and hands together as if she'd just come in from the outside, blows on her fingers. She closes her eyes momentarily, and tics replace the stretched agony of staring. Breathe, breathe, shallow, breathe, deep.

Tonight she did not turn on the light.

WHEN Annie was small, she had had a recurring dream about a wave. She would be standing on the beach in Sandy Cove, when all of a sudden far out to sea, a huge wave would start to build. At first she could just make it out, the sea's surface gone wrong, then she would see it advance, a wall of water. Annie would be frozen to the spot, her feet stuck in the sand, as the water came toward her. She would know that the wave would suck her out to sea, drown her. The dream always ended with Annie forcing herself to wake, screaming at that very moment when the wave had blocked her vision of everything—the horizon, the sea, the rocks with their tidal pools, the beach at her feet.

One night a voice inside her, angelic or demonic but compelling, had told Annie to just wait, let the wave come. And as the wave and the dream began to build, she had waited, although it was hard to believe in the voice instead of the wave. The wave had come, enveloped her, left her standing there unharmed, laughing. The sensation had been pleasurable, nothing more than a great splash that left her tingling. Then the dream itself had dissolved, and it never came back.

Annie tried to use the same strategy to deal with the beast who inhabited her dark room, but it did no good. The more she let it come, the more it took advantage, the longer it stayed.

"MY feeling is that what you've experienced is a panic attack," Alice MacKay told her when she made an appointment at the nursing station. "Panic attacks are quite common. A lot of people have them from time to time. Usually they occur because of some stress, a source of anxiety, worry or fear that has been suppressed. Specific situations can trigger attacks. Do you know what could be causing yours?"

"No."

"There's nothing new—nothing going on that's bothering you?"

"No."

"Maybe you just need a vacation, a break. But you won't be getting one of those for a while. What about sick leave? You could take sick leave and go out for a while, home, perhaps, or even somewhere you've never been."

"I couldn't do that. What would everybody think? Oh, I can just hear it now—everyone would say I cracked up."

"Perhaps they would. Perhaps they wouldn't. If they did, you'd come back and prove them wrong, anyway. So who cares?"

"I care. Anyway, I can't leave the students up in the air like that. It's too late in the year, too much work to be done."

"You don't think anyone else could do the work—just temporarily?"

"That's not the point."

"I see. Okay, tell you what: I can give you a mild sedative. Maybe if you're really ready to sleep when you go to bed, you will be able to avoid the anxiety build-up. Okay? Take two about an hour before bedtime. Two should do it. If you find that's too much, if you're groggy in the morning, reduce the dosage to one."

"I don't know. I hate taking drugs."

"The alternative?"

"Yes, well."

ANNIE takes the pills faithfully, and for a week the beast stays away. One night she feels it stir, picks out its vague outline by the moonlit window, but she is blissfully asleep before she can consider if it will come any closer.

The next week, something odd happens. Annie takes the pills as she usually does, but she stays half-awake for a long time in a trance-like, dreamy state. She feels a great desire to talk, and no desire at all to go to bed. Instead, she stays in the living room talking to Marian or Sheila, or anyone else who might be around. She talks to them across a great distance, in slow motion, and she knows that her voice is slurring. Eventually, at their insistence, she goes to bed.

ON the sofa, Marian glances at Sheila. What is she on? their looks seem to say. Is she losing it? For three nights now, Marian and Sheila have had to turn off all the lights and go to bed whether they wanted to or not just to get Annie to go, get her to stop this incessant talk which trails on and on, jumping from subject to subject in a way they cannot follow.

Finally, one night, Annie sees the look that passes between them and interprets it. She goes to bed in a rage, thinks of tossing the pills in the toilet, remembers that she would have to carry a bucket of water up the stairs to flush them, then stuffs them in a dresser drawer full of undeveloped film, bank statements, and all-occasion cards.

WITHOUT the pills, without the comforting promise of sleep, Annie lies in the dark and waits for the beast to come. I'm having a nervous breakdown, that's what this is, a goddam nervous breakdown, it's been waiting for me all these years.

ANNIE'S mother had had a nervous breakdown once, right after Joy was born. Annie had been eight. Every time Annie remembers it, she can taste the terror. The terror tastes like the tinned corned beef and beans and wieners eaten during her mother's absence. She had *lost* her mother for a whole month, and after that, Annie didn't have a lot of faith in things. Everything seemed easily broken, the things you trusted most of all could change, and there was nothing you could do about it. Annie's father had taken time off work, stayed home with them, tried to make the whole thing seem like a big adventure demanding ingenuity, courage, daring. For a few days, they had felt tough and adventurous, like the Swiss Family Robinson or something. But when Annie's mother didn't return after a week, the whole thing started to fall apart. There had been hair-pulling, snivelling, threats to run away, refusals to eat. The baby, Joy, cried all the time; her face was full of snot, she smelled bad. Annie and her sisters had had to walk her back and forth in an endless trek through the kitchen to keep her quiet. It was the first time Annie had seen her father lose his temper.

In Annie's mind forever there is a picture of her mother before she left for the hospital—standing by the fridge, smoking a cigarette. A plastic bowl full of dish water had been slowly melting on a burner on the stove. Annie saw the vacant look in her mother's eyes, how they ignored the bowl and seemed fixed on something out in the meadow, was terrified, and she sent her younger brother Stephen to go get dad at the sawmill, hurry, hurry, don't just stand there, drop that truck and hurry!

Afterwards, the family never spoke of what had happened. Once Annie's mother got well, that was that. And Joy didn't even know about it. Annie's mother had been afraid that Joy would blame herself.

I'M having a nervous breakdown, yes, Annie thinks. Like Mom did. Things just fall apart for no reason. Things you don't even think about build up, everything falls apart. Annie is filled with anger and bitterness. In the seven years she has taught, Annie has done everything right. She is meticulous in her work. She always looks professional. She takes care to do things right, right to the last detail, the constantly changing displays on her classroom walls testimonials to her awareness of every seasonal shift, holiday, news item. She cares about the children in her classrooms, cares about them more than she has to, never forgets them. Years later, she would recognize their faces anywhere. I don't deserve this, she thinks, I don't deserve it.

DARKNESS. Annie can feel the advance of the beast as surely as she once felt the advance of the wave. Over there, by the curtains, it stretches its dark body, limbering up for the attack. The curtains move slightly as if pushed. Annie decides to sleep with the light on. The beast, she knows, is a creation of the darkness, feeding on the absence of light, taking courage from the insomniac's altered vision and insecurity. It lives in that crevice of consciousness between sleep and wakefulness. Annie lies with the bedside lamp on. The room is now safe and familiar, almost without shadows. She knows that in that brightly lit room she won't be able to sleep for a long time, that when she wakes her eyes will be red, as from crying or drinking, from the strain of exposure to the bright light.

Annie wonders if someone will walk by at this late hour—or even later—and notice the light shining through her window.

She pictures someone walking home, wonders if he will stop to light a cigarette, look up, think it odd, and perhaps later mention to someone else how some people sure stay up late at night when they got to go to work early in the morning.

Perhaps someone will look for the telltale dark marks under her eyes. Perhaps if the beast continues this assault all winter, Annie will come to be known as that odd woman, nearly thirty, who is afraid of the dark. A little bit of her secret life is shining out of here, out onto the snow, a signal to be picked up by any passerby.

February 02

I got my plane ticket in the mail today. I'll be leaving on the 12th of the month and returning on the 17th. A lot of the time will be spent in transit. First Goose Bay, overnight. Then Deer Lake. Taxi to Corner Brook. I'm staying at the Glynmill Inn, too early for the swans on the pond, too early for leaves on the encircling trees, but time enough to look out the window and feel that there are more people living around me than I could fit in a large banquet hall.

When I left home and went to university, I stood one day in a line-up, and suddenly I realized that there were more people in the line-up than there were in the outport I'd come from. I was seized by panic, felt nauseous and disembodied, and thought all of a sudden that I wouldn't be able to handle it. Every year, kids from outports tried and didn't handle it. They'd go home, work in the fish plant, get married. All there would be of the thing they'd planned for years was the memory of a few days of discomfort. It wasn't going to happen to me. Eventually, I stopped feeling lost all the time.

This place has had the opposite effect. I feel closed in, surrounded, and it almost makes you feel crazy to think that you could feel closed in amid such vast open space. But I had become unused to the fishbowl effect, the sense that you'd better watch yourself, not slip up; everyone knows what you're up to, whether you are up to something or nothing at all.

The trip out also saves me the Valentine parties. Everyone is having one. I even promised my Grade Ten class a party if they all finished Romeo and Juliet by Valentine's Day. They said they couldn't understand it. I told them that anyone who could follow a soap opera could understand Romeo and Juliet. Besides, I told them, I'm not asking you to understand it, just read it. They reminded me that I wouldn't even be there to know if they finished or not. I said I had Cupid watching them, but I know only two or three will finish it, and then someone asked me who Cupid was.

Perhaps I will rewrite Romeo and Juliet for them. The families will hate each other because one of the forefathers drowned fishing in the other's boat, and the survivor has been held responsible ever since. Perhaps the two men had once wanted the same woman, or were in dispute over the paternity of a child. Something everyday and tragic like that. There will be no balcony, but a rendezvous in a camp in the woods. Someone will see them, and the jig will be up. There will be guns instead of daggers.

February 04
Storm. You would think the devil had gotten into the wind. The walls of this pre-fab house have taken in the wind. Somewhere between the interior and exterior walls, the wind is expanding, a creature puffed up with its own breath and furious energy, waiting for enough strength to blow the house apart. This has been going on since yesterday, and now I'm just hoping that the electricity won't go, that the furnace won't go out.

Dave Marshall says he's glad he didn't get a water bed, because one morning he and his guest would wake up frozen to a king-sized hockey rink. Guest, he said, as if he's entertaining there all the time.

Dave ruins it: he shot us all meaningful glances, so we all knew he was full of it.

I can just barely hear them talking now, Dave and Rudy and Annie and Marian, down with the picture window heaving in and out as if it will shatter itself.

Carl has been bringing Marian presents. Now that she's not leaving, he's trying to woo her back. He brought her a clock: now where did he get that? It's an old-fashioned one that you have to wind up, and it ticks loudly and chimes the hours. Carl making his presence felt with his souvenir ticking away, telling her: carpe diem. I hate the sound of a clock ticking in a house. It reminds me of my grandparents' house on Sunday afternoons. Everyone was always bored and unhappy there. They wouldn't let themselves work on Sundays, and work was the only thing they felt comfortable doing.

February 05

Third day of storm. The school finally closed. There were ice crystals in the air. It's dangerous to breathe them; they can cut your lungs like ground glass.

I was doing all right for a while, but tonight I took out a bottle of wine and I'm starting to slip. I was trying not to; I've seen too many things ruined by a bottle. I'm up in bed wrapped up in the blanket, drinking by myself. There's not much water left; we haven't been able to get any since the storm started. I feel dirty, would like a bath. Oh, the taps in the Glynmill Inn will run like cataracts when I get there. Christ, I wish I could sleep.

February 06

White swirl of snow
Enfolds us, time holds us
Rigid. No night.
No day. No decay.
White-out.

February 07

It's over. The wind finally wore itself out. I have a crashing
hangover; all day it's been a swizzle stick in my brain. I've got to
get down to see Peggy. I've started to rely on her to keep me sane.
She has this calming effect on me. The only way I can express it is:
she knows how to live.

Now, how does she know how to do that?

It's getting close to trip time. The kids are plying me with requests to
bring back records and tapes. Someone — I can't remember who —
wants a set of Wedgwood Blue placemats to match the rest of her
kitchen. I've got a big booze order to get. I'm taking a bag of dirty
clothes with me, and a couple of outfits from the Cinderella closet.
I took them out already and sized them up. They look pretty silly.
I must have had really bad taste last year.

February 10

Letter from Derek. He's getting married. Her name is Annabelle
Stewart—sounds like a descendant of royalty. Aunt Letitia will be
pleased that the family line won't be sullied by any opportunistic
little Micks from around the bay.

I must say I've been expecting this. Tonight, I made him a card with a guy shooting at a hockey puck with "Happy Rebound" on it. Is that right — or are rebounds in basketball? I wonder if Annabelle Stewart is a sports fan. Oh well, we're all sports fans in the beginning. It's only later we learn to say what we love and hate.

On Saturday

T HIS SATURDAY, Alice moves between cursing the people whose ailments and accidents are the very reason for her job and condemning herself because she feels that way. Three of the injuries she has seen today, all reluctant emergencies unwilling to show themselves to her scrutiny, were either directly or indirectly the result of last night's blow-out. A plane carrying two passengers and six cases of liquor, ordered in spurts but arriving all at once, had angled in on a red sunset with a howling wind whipping up ferocious tails of snow which beat the land, and anyone moving over it, into submission.

Hunched figures had hurtled toward the airstrip, faces bent low, grimacing behind windscreens. It was the kind of cold that made you feel that your hide had been hauled back, that you'd been skinned like a rabbit. The wind had gone straight through coats and snowsuits and gloves to the tender flesh underneath. It was a day to cower under. Alice had gone to the airstrip expecting a load of medical supplies for the nursing station, basic things, things she couldn't wait for, that and four bottles of wine and one of Grand Marnier.

The plane had sidled in, tipping and wheeling like a blown kite, buffeted by the wind, then, something obviously wrong with the landing gear, had shimmied at a frightful speed down the expanse of icy gravel, and just at the margin, had somehow stopped. People who had held their breaths suddenly let them go, filling the air with a mist that froze instantly. Alice often thought when she saw this that if, as some people believed, the breath was the soul, then in this climate one would be able to see the departing soul hanging in the air, a frozen soul, crystallized proof that we are more than flesh and blood.

But Alice didn't believe in souls anymore, had seen too many bodies dead, mangled, mutilated or wrecked into final submission to believe that they contained more than what she could see. She had seen bodies opened, giving up all their secrets until there was no mystery left except how the person had held on so long. She had seen bodies cave in on themselves, leaving a husk with nothing, no room for a soul in between. No, Alice was a medical person, scientific in her logic, direct in her approach. She could not mend souls so she ignored them; what was needed was help for the cancerous lung, the severed finger, the tipped uterus. Alice left souls to Mr George and Mr Graham, the self-proclaimed purveyors of spiritual things.

So Alice, as soon as the plane had come to its wavering stop, had rushed out to meet it. There might be injuries. There were none. And there was Emilie Mitsuk, walking down the steps with a broad smile on her face, holding her newborn, greeting everyone as if nothing had happened. Emilie had been waiting for days for a plane to take her home; she had probably hardly noticed the rough landing.

That night, at assorted parties around the community, the marvel had been that, in all the bumping and skidding and veering, not a single bottle had been broken. The partiers toasted the pilots, applauding their skill and ingenuity; everybody wanted them at their particular party. And they toasted Emilie and her baby, Emilie for not being scared at all, and the baby for the hope that all babies hold out to the dry and tired and the sick-of-it-all. Emilie was naming the baby Whitney, after her favourite singer, and everyone except the older women agreed it was a strong name.

The pilots, having to remain to wait for help to fix the broken plane tomorrow, took the night off and managed, in their shining newfound heroism, to find two girls who, coming from small families, had bedrooms of their own.

And now the weather was coming down, and the plane would not be leaving today. Alice looked at the girl on the bed, her round child's face disfigured behind a film of pain and sweat. The plane had been a godsend for the girl. She would get out, get expert attention. But now she would have to wait.

"How are you?" Alice murmurs, becoming motherly, reluctantly maternal to this girl who'd been in her office last year with a case of something nasty her boyfriend had brought back from one of his trips to the world he referred to as 'civilization' whenever he got out to a broomball tournament or a rock concert.

"Any better?" Alice puts her large hand on the girl's taut stomach.

"It's not supposed to be—not supposed to be like this. I'm only seven and a half months gone," the girl entreats in a voice that begs to be told that this is a bad dream, a nightmare illness from eating too much chocolate or fresh meat.

She will wake and the nightmare will be over; it will be a shining Monday morning and the little girl will meet Sissy and Brenda and Jacqui by the town hall and they'll walk to school, making plans for the dance next Saturday night and betting on who Erica will finally choose to love forever in the beautiful candlelit evenings of her soap opera world. They will talk about what she will be wearing when she finally tells him she loves him, forsaking all others. And they'll get the chance to talk about it in class; the teacher will surely use Friday's episode to talk about something in literature, like the day she used it to talk about dramatic tension.

The teacher has given up fighting about their watching the stories, and they're glad; it seemed strange anyway, the young teacher with no interest in love. Lydia tries to think of what Erica would do now, what she might say to the nurse. But Erica was never fat and pregnant; in real life, she might have had a baby but Lydia doubted it: a magazine had said that she was only ninety-eight pounds.

In her haze of pain, Lydia is diminishing, becoming smaller, until she is a girl before falling in love and boyfriends and periods even, a little girl who couldn't be pregnant. She does that a lot now, goes back.

Alice finds a cool cloth to place on the girl's brow.

"Would you like me to pull the shades?" she asks. The heavy yellowish beige blinds plunge the room into a curious yellow-grey sea, the colour of candlelit funeral parlours, dinners for two, or the light over the sea before a storm. But they block out the storm coming, the outside relentlessly breaking the promise that Alice had made to the frightened girl earlier in the morning. It's going to be clear today, the forecast says, and the pilots should have the plane ready by one o'clock. But it's two already, and outside the weather is coming down.

"No, leave them open," Lydia says. "It's nice to be able to see out. There goes Sissy from the post office. She must have got the money to get her parcel out." Lydia lapses into silence followed by a long sigh. "Sissy's boyfriend told her that if she lost twenty pounds she'd look just like a movie star, and he'd get her some new clothes. Then he didn't get his unemployment so she had to wait. Good thing they didn't send the parcel back. She ordered three pairs of cords and four new sweaters—and a dress for the darts banquet."

Alice looks at Sissy hurrying by, the heavy parcel clasped in her arms snug around the brown wrapper, long dark hair streaming out behind her. Alice catches a glimpse of Sissy's happy face, red with cold, new clothes to look at and try on before the storm moves in.

"It's probably only false labour, anyway," Alice says, but the taut stomach affronts her, calls her bluff, proclaims readiness and immediacy.

Alice wishes that Lydia would let her pull the shades. Outside, along the opposite shore where on clear days the distinct outline of a woman lying on her side can be made out in the rocks pushing against the sky, the tops of the hills have already begun to disappear. The Woman On The Hill is becoming indistinct now; her great head, massive shoulders, the hand under her jaw and the jutting breasts are veiled with snow. Only the broad curve of her side and the powerful legs are still visible.

Lydia must know. The horizon is a feather pillow, stuffed to the breaking point—the horizon, like poor Lydia, threatening to let go before the appointed time, a storm not supposed to break until Sunday, a baby not to be born for another month and a half.

The nursing station is almost empty. The others with their problems at least temporarily mended, have all gone home. Jimmy MacLean had fallen on a bottle and cut his arm. Not a bad one, but requiring stitches. It had happened at five o'clock, or thereabouts, and Jimmy had sat heroically in the circle of drinking men with his arm tied up in the improvised tourniquet of a towel until six, the wound bleeding slowly, the gash unnerving him more and more.

"It's gettin' some blue," Bill Roberts had warned him, watching Jimmy for signs of fear. Finally, Jimmy had given in and gone to the station "to have it looked at." That was what they always said, "Nurse, could you take a look at my arm—my foot, my privates, my head, my knee, my guts, my eyes…" As if a look would help somehow, although Alice was well aware of how reassuring a look could be. People went home satisfied: "I had the nurse take a look at it," they would say.

So Alice looked. At Jimmy's torn arm, at a lavender frozen foot. At a black eye swollen almost shut. "He was jealous of me," the woman said proudly, as if to be desired enough to arouse jealousy at her age was proof against any amount of pain, any suffering that might be inflicted upon her body, swollen as it was from her rich bread, her boiled dinners unrivalled in the sheer padding they could put on your bones against the cold months.

"Why do you put up with it?" Alice had asked her once in a moment of boiling anger, after Margie had come in with a cracked rib.

"He's a good man, he is, only when he gets drinking he gets like that. He thinks I'm fooling around when he's drinking. He thinks all the men have got their eyes on me. Just waiting their chance. But…he don't drink often."

127

Yet, in six years, Alice has ministered to almost every inch of Margie's body, until for her now it was a catalogue of bruises, a chronology of abuse, a textbook case.

And all the time she had been talking to Margie, this girl, Lydia, had hovered in the hall, bent a little, white-faced, waiting for her turn, too polite to rush in. Finally she had slumped in the chair, hands clutched over her swollen stomach, and Alice had caught her eye.

"Miss MacKay, it can't be but it feels like the baby's coming."

"We'll get you out on the plane today," Alice had said after examining her, hoping that it was false labour, knowing that her hopes in such instances were usually deflated by some kind of accursed fate that made her assurances turn to tragedy and her bright words become tired condolences offered too late.

Alice is tired of saying "If only..." and "You should..." She'd heard about Lydia from her teacher, and from the social worker Lydia wouldn't see. For she had categorically denied her pregnancy, had worn jeans right up to the point where she had to lie on the bed and suck in her stomach to close them, had said she had a stomach bug that she couldn't get rid of, had played hockey until the other girls finally got her to stop. She had even speculated that she might have some kind of growth, something dark and dangerous. To get it removed, she would have to go off to a hospital far away, the only hospital where the surgery could be performed.

Lydia had thought a lot at night about the hospital. All the doctors would be so handsome and so clean in their white coats, and there would be flowers on the table beside her bed. Her surgery would be very dangerous, but she would be saved. There would be a hunk of a doctor named Brad.

But not pregnant. She wouldn't be pregnant. Not having babies, not at fifteen, not like her mother who was still having babies.

"Perhaps," Jacqui had said in one of her nasty moods, "Your mother will have another baby and then you'll have a baby older than your brother or sister. How neat!"

Jacqui had thought that would be interesting, something different, but not that different, certainly not in Jacqui's family. Jacqui's mother and her oldest daughters had babies almost the same age. Jacqui's mother had had eight in all. The house was full of babies.

And in the beginning for a long time Lydia had sailed by in her own world, insulating herself, hoping that it was all a mistake and she could be herself again, could banish this unwelcome change, believing as always in the power of wishes.

She had wanted not to be grown up suddenly. She had stopped wearing so much makeup, she was sorry she had wanted sexy, grown-up clothes, cuddling in every night with a small and dilapidated bear, growing into herself, becoming small. Some nights she had cried in the dark, muffled by the heavy blankets. Still, the baby grew, larger and more terrifying each day. And Lydia didn't know what she would do when the baby was born. She'd thought she'd have more time. Something might happen. They all lied. They said it would be nine months. It would be soon.

❋ ❋ ❋

LULLABIES come to Alice's mind as she watches the girl, uncharacteristic of her to remember such songs. It was a year ago that Alice had sat across the desk from Lydia, suggesting to her in the hesitant way that a nurse might suggest to a fourteen-year-old girl, that it might be a good idea if she went on the pill. But Lydia had denied doing anything she might need a pill for. "We only fools around," she'd said defensively, giving Alice a look that suggested she'd better not pry, not ask any further, just give her something to get rid of the thing he'd brought back from the broomball tournament in Gander, a place that Lydia hates already because it made him betray her. "There's other ways of getting *that*," Lydia had insisted when Alice had given her a knowing look.

Lydia can't get the two things together in her mind, the far-off world that television gives her where love and romance are everywhere and people dress up and have cocktails every day. It can't be the same world Harry goes out to, the world he came back from with the awful thing that made her pee burn and smell bad. She didn't know; she'd never been outside. But when she thought of that world, she'd always thought of it as so *clean*. And she wouldn't do it with Harry anymore. She'd show him; if you loved someone, you didn't go out on them.

So the pills stayed in Alice's cupboard. Alice had boxes of them; she didn't think of them so much as birth control but as poverty control. The older women would take them readily, knowing from the weight of long experience the reality of poverty, the stretchy dollar that never pulled far enough, stamps always running out before the fishing season began, the sparse cupboard in early spring, hands reaching out to empty it as soon as it was filled. Winter could be a nightmare, the gnawing hunger that makes you fat, eating all the time in fear that there would be nothing to eat sooner or later. So the older women take the pills and go, preferring the risk of stroke to the risk of pregnancy.

But the young girls with their beautiful fresh faces will not touch the pills. There is no danger. Pregnancy is for mothers. For sisters. But not for them.

"Miss, could I have a glass of water or something?"

"How about a Coke?" knowing that Lydia likes Coke.

"Oh yes, good." She is beaming, the surprise of strict Alice having a stash of Coke, not some awful juice made from crushed carrots or something such as Lydia would expect a nurse to have. When Alice did nutrition classes at school, she looked so stern you'd think she'd punish you personally for not eating the right things.

"It's getting worse, isn't it?" Lydia indicates the window with her head as Alice hands her the Coke. Alice follows her expression to the outside, not wanting to look into the girl's eyes, eyes demanding truth. The sky is a contusion, full of flaring purples and sickly yellow-greys like dead skin. Along the horizon, a red glow edges the bruise, as if exerting pressure. Wind eddies, small conical storms with dancing sprites in their centres, swoosh over the snow, low to the ground, a dance to invite the horrible sky closer, closer, to fill the middle space with stinging bone-chilling frenzy. In an hour, maybe less, the middle space will be a fine unbreathable powder like chalk dust.

Alice will not lie anymore. "If they don't get the plane out by three, they won't be able to go today." Alice moves closer. "Ssshh, listen, I think it's going to be all right. You won't be having that baby today, maybe not for a while yet, but certainly not today. Okay?"

Alice tries to believe her own words, wondering to what degree she has probably exchanged one lie for another, a comfort given for a comfort removed. Like digging a hole and, looking into its blackness, filling it in immediately. Withdraw a comfort, give another; it is the philosophy of minimal pain, feeding things too terrible to be taken wholly in small, bite-sized pieces. Take a little of the poison regularly and nobody will be able to kill you with it.

Amy, the relief nurse, won't be here until four. Alice needs sleep and a bath, and now, sitting here in this room filled with pain and fatigue and the promise of storm, she thinks that perhaps she should not go out tonight, should stay here with the girl. Amy's so new, and she finds it difficult to talk to these girls, is afraid, even, when she has to stay at the nursing station alone; she thinks someone will come to rob her or molest her. Not here, Alice could tell her, anywhere else but here.

I'll go, she decides. That's what I always tell them: don't get too involved. Empathize, but take your time off. Otherwise, you'll be sorry—later. Take your own medicine, she tells herself, and just to be sure, she takes a painkiller for the headache guilt never fails to give her.

＊　＊　＊

THE women's party. As she dresses, Alice thinks of the prospect with a mixture of anticipation and premature boredom. Difficult when you know what everyone's going to say already. How it will progress. How it will end. But she'd started the damn things, tired, disgusted with the male obsession with Saturday night hockey, the women quieted, feigning interest until midnight and not opening their mouths. She'd started the alternative, and she'd better go. Lord knows, the women need it, she thinks, a diversion away from the men. And she didn't like the way things always ended in small communities; the one who was originally interested gave up, and the rest followed suit. Then, there was nothing to do again.

The women's parties were rituals. The men at their hockey game, their version of the secret society with its ceremonies and passwords. The men's game, the women's party. The politics of semi-peaceful coexistence. There's a woman land claims specialist here for the weekend. God, Alice thinks, new blood, someone new to talk to. Alice looks forward to it the way some people look forward to vacations.

THE women have gotten dressed up again. White blouses with high necks and string ties. Pullovers, dress pants, curls. It goes with the margaritas and martinis being made so skilfully in the kitchen that one would think that these teachers spend their apprenticeships for their jobs working in bars. The young one, Sheila, admits to it. She's a born bartender. Introduce me, introduce me, Alice says.

The land claims specialist's name is Janice Barton. Alice likes the look of her, a no-nonsense woman, yet not hard and brittle around the edges. But, it turns out, she has an idealized view of the north. Her eyes go soft and misty when she talks about "the people," and she uses the word Inuit, Alice knows, in its original meaning. "The people." Then who the hell, Alice would like to say, are the rest of us? But she can't trade the conversation for truth, can't bite in. Janice has a law degree. From Dalhousie. She notices how much the women are drinking. Do they always drink like this? She knew that alcoholism was a problem in the north, but she thought it was largely confined to...

Alice watches Janice blush, caught in the trap of her own biases. "Believe me, Janice, this is not alcohol abuse. This is a break. That's all. A housewives' vacation. Therapy."

She goes off to the kitchen to freshen her glass of wine but, through the partition, she cannot help watching the new woman. And all the while she knows she must talk to the others. But it's boring! The awful boredom of knowing the same words have been said at a gathering two weeks ago, last year, when was it? Endless repetitions, additions, nuances.

"Did you hear..."

"If I won the 649..."

"The best coconut squares I ever made..."

"The sexiest man on television..."

"Oh, I can't do nothing about *my* hips..."

She wishes that one time, just once, she could get at what is really in their minds, beyond recipes for cut glass squares (which Alice refuses to eat because of their reference to internal bleeding), beyond diets and the possibility of getting a few of them together to do the Jane Fonda workout tape on a regular basis so that their breasts and bellies and bums will not droop in premature attrition, beyond husbands and children's diseases and making your own beer and references to erotic fantasy encounters with soap opera stars.

Alice knows that the women think about other things, but will not say. It's the same everywhere, she thinks—women! There are many times in her life when Alice would just as soon not be a woman. It implied too many things she couldn't stomach.

Alice wonders if any of the other women here are, like her, lovers of women. Secretly. For in any other place Alice would have a strong woman at her side, and they would shop on Saturdays at open markets and buy books and feast on pasta and wine on a city balcony in late evening. Here she is a soother, pacifier. "Come to me, all of you who labour and are overburdened." It was not the sort of role where one could create havoc in the sexual order.

Most of Alice's women friends say that lesbians give them the creeps. Would they let her touch them, their daughters, if they knew? It is an odd intimacy, Alice thinks; once you look at a body in weakness, in submission, it's too late to change the rules. If she was going to continue to help them, she'd better not upset them, send them away.

From the corner of her eye she watches Janice Barton, deep in conversation with Frances Hope about coconut balls. Janice Barton, Alice knows, is the sort of woman who contains in her memory carefully sorted files, repertoires of conversations so that she knows just what to say to everyone. Coconut balls! You can tell by looking at her that Janice Barton has never been within sniffing distance of condensed milk.

"I didn't know coconuts had balls, Francie," Margie pokes Frances in the ribs, giggling, as she passes by.

"I wanted to tell you about the shower for young Lydia." Margie is standing in front of Alice now.

"Shower?"

"Yes, girl, we gotta have a shower for her. For the new baby."

Oh, Christ, Alice thinks, that's all they can think about, bloody showers. And Lydia, how is she now? And when this is over, one way or another, what will Lydia need? Someone to tell her to stay in school, to take care of herself, to love herself as no one else will. But who is there for such guidance? Alice tries to retrace the dark steps of history to a time when the older women were the wise ones who gave guidance to the young, but she cannot imagine it. Lydia lying in pain and they're planning a bloody shower.

Alice had gone to a few of these showers before. You sort of had to, but she found it embarrassing. How many clothespins can you pick up to win the game? How fast can you put underwear on over your outside clothes, without using your hands? At showers, these were the sort of games women played. They tried to be playful but, pathetically, had forgotten how. Real play was what you did with your babies if you had the time.

Standing in the hall doorway, Alice realizes what she has done. She has done this at every party she has attended lately. Slowly, her mind wills itself into the lonely exercise of criticism, until she is truly outside and has no option but to leave. She is, after all, in the doorway. Always the distance, she thinks, the distance.

She will watch and wait with Lydia tonight. There probably isn't really any need to, but Alice thinks of the girl alone in the dark, remembers herself at that age, and thinks of how sad it is to be fifteen even if you aren't pregnant and alone and ill and frightened. This night, to Lydia, will be an eternity.

AMY looks up quickly when Alice arrives, clearly relieved. "You can go now. I'll take over."

"Her water has broken. I just called Mina to come and assist. She used to be a midwife. I was just about to call you. Oh, and I'll stay."

"Thanks."

Lydia's eyes are squeezed shut. She has retreated even further into herself. Alice knows that she will have to draw her out for this to work.

The eyes, when they open, are still veiled with hurt and surprise, but Alice can see in their dark shining centres an incredible, desperate courage. She passes a smile to Lydia, and begins to time the contractions, begins the countdown of birth.

"Lydia, Lydia," she calls, willing her to come out, *come out and be positive, come out and begin the adventure of your new life.* She repeats the words silently and rubs the girl's hands. Over a long and private distance, Lydia's eyes slowly pass unknown landscapes until they arrive at the present, the room, Alice, the pain.

March 02

I haven't been able to write for awhile. I went out to the conference, came back, and was behind in everything. Tests and papers just seem to pile up, up, up, and now I have to really get serious about preparing the senior class for final exams. Public exams — a terror for them. We've been told that it's important to get more passing results every year. Once the students were forced out of their communities to a boarding school to finish high school. A lot of them hated it, couldn't take the loneliness on top of the pressure. Now, we all have to work to justify the decision to keep them in their communities.

The conference. Three days of sitting around tables, cute getting-acquainted exercises to start the sessions, then long afternoons followed by restaurant dinners. I had forgotten how much I missed restaurants, that feeling of being indulged, tended on. And the change was nice except that I felt anxious the whole time. As if someone would discover that I didn't belong.

I got my hair done the first day I got out. Did my laundry. And the baths! Soaking in the tub, mounds of bubbles everywhere. Soft white towels. And no clean-up after, let alone hauling water!

I missed two conference sessions because I was soaking in the tub. I feel guilty because I know it was expensive to send me there. But it's a delicious guilt. I even had strawberries, and I brought back bags of fresh fruit. It was funny—when I got back, the way the fruit made everyone so happy, no, not just happy, more like raptured, ecstatic, orgasmic. Especially Peggy — you should see her eat a peach when she hasn't had one for a while. What a spoiled lot we are, really.

Of course there was some man trouble while I was out there. The thing wouldn't be complete without man trouble. Down in the bar on the second night, I ran into Brendan Halfyard, an old friend of Derek's from university. Brendan's from Corner Brook, and when I asked him what he was doing back home, he said he'd gotten a job in a small technical sales company. Commerce graduate — all through university, he looked as though he'd already had his hair cut for the job interview.

We ended up talking about Derek, and Brendan looked at me meaningfully and said that he thought Derek didn't know when he had a good thing, and some guys should be so lucky. I knew right then and there that he wanted to sleep with me. But I couldn't. There's something raw inside me that I just want to keep to myself. So I kept fending him off, changing the subject. And then he got kind of subtly abusive, like he wanted to put me down because I wasn't interested. I've seen that before. So I ended up drinking alone in my room like I said I wasn't going to.

Maybe I should have slept with Brendan, though, because I spent the rest of the time examining learning modules and wondering if I wanted to go home. And wondering where home was.

Lydia had her baby. It's hard to believe that such a small girl could have a baby. Apparently, they had a rough go of it, but they're both okay.

March 11

Carl's here a lot now—too much. Marian doesn't know what to do: she walks the floor half the night, from window to window like a ghost looking for an exit to another dimension. Carl's told her his field work is almost done; he'll leave when the ice breaks up if she wants.

The other night she told me a weird story about Carl. Last spring, when she agreed to come here with him, they had come up to do some preliminary work, and they had travelled to another community by skidoo. It was late May. They were travelling over sea ice, and Marian had become frightened because the sun and warm air had started to melt the surface of the ice, and the skis of their borrowed machines were swishing through slush. The ice was yellow or blackish in places. Although the ice had to be feet thick, and Carl had reassured her that it was, Marian didn't feel safe. She begged him to turn back, to let them go by plane, but he wouldn't. He just kept going faster, and she had to follow him or get lost. She said that she kept her eyes on the red gas can on his komatik, and she just looked at that and nothing else, all the way. She was too scared to look up or down.

When they got to the community, Carl had said that, see — nothing happened, did it? All she had to do was trust him, not give in to her stupid fears.

Then she asked me if I would trust someone who would do that.

March 17

I got a card from Angela with a leprechaun on it. And a letter from the school board. The letter asks me if I'm staying or going — next year, that is. At least they're not firing me, so I suppose I must be doing my job right.

Everybody got the same letter. Annie's staying. Dave doesn't know—hinted that he might have other prospects. Rudy doesn't know; he said that maybe he wouldn't write back, and then the board could decide where to put him. I don't know what I'm going to do.

One part of me wants to get out, go somewhere more familiar, go someplace where I can get in a car and leave for the weekend if I feel like it. That's the hardest part, not being able to leave at all. We've got until the end of the month to decide, but that doesn't seem like much time.

Every time I think about leaving, I think about my students. I actually like them, and that's the biggest surprise about teaching. I feel like they've just gotten to know me, and here I am considering leaving them to deal with another stranger. But perhaps they're not getting the best from me anyhow, just the best I can give at the moment. I wonder if I need them more than they need me?

March 22

I've written two letters. One says that I'm leaving, the other says I'm staying. I keep taking them out and shifting them around on the desk with my eyes closed, to see which one comes out on top. I shuffle them like cards, whispering "Abracadabra," as if magic will merge the two choices into some better reality.

But I know this is foolishness — I'll have to make my mind up soon. And this is not a good time, because although March is the stormiest month here, it is also the time when you see the very first signs of spring, days that trick you into thinking there's a real thaw coming, days when the sun is a soft, slow burn, and icicles begin to drip on the eaves of the school.

I have to keep remembering January — going to work in darkness, leaving in darkness, the only hours of light confined to working indoors. The hum of the fluorescent lights at two in the afternoon. The darkness inside a storm, like the darkness inside a fire must be.

Of course, I still wonder if I'll end up an alcoholic if I stay. But then there's no assurance I won't end up one anywhere else. Anyway, shuffle-shuffle, let it wait.

Outside my classroom, the icicles are doing their slow drip. Frost glitters in the sun. I have sixty tests to correct, and some have been on my desk for a week. The copier is on the blink again. Everyone tells me to just wait and see—spring is really beautiful here.

Coming Back from the Shenak

RUDY CONNOLLY sat in the middle of a howl, a buzz, a crowd of men, and perfected his ritual. Rudy's was a ritual of disgust; first he'd take the bottle in hand, wincing at the label that proclaimed gut-rot whisky, then he'd bring the bottle close, close, draw his eyebrows together in consternation, and pour the whisky. This done, he reached for the plastic jug on the table. The jug contained powdered lemonade and water and sugar and had a small granular sediment in the bottom. Rudy took the jug, looked offended, and shook it. Some of it spilled on his pants. Rudy wiped his pants with the back of his hand, feeling the granular, sugary liquid stick to the hairs there. Then he reached for the ice-cube tray. The ice cubes, long out of the freezer and into the fire of a heated conversation about hockey, were half-melted and sodden. A brownish mineral residue hung in suspension in a brackish melt. Rudy shook six of the half-cubes into his drink, grimaced and pulled back. There...there...there...

"Fuckin' little faggot's all he is..." Ed was saying, as his pet hate, the Great Wayne Gretzky, glided across the screen, cool and slim and unbruised. Ed's voice rose, launching into a litany of praise for the New York Islanders.

A lone voice rose from a corner to defend the Montreal Canadiens, and was quickly silenced; they'd won too many Stanley Cups to get any sympathy here.

An older man began to mourn the untimely demise of the Toronto Maple Leafs, his drunken, halting rambling harkening back to the days of battery radios. But over all a feeling of general lassitude hung. They were waiting, although they'd never admit it, for the women.

The women were at the residence of one Alice MacKay, a nurse with a formidable girth, an unchallenged smile, and a manner that would dismiss a multitude of Hockey Night in Canada viewers.

Faced with the prospect of being sshhed into silence every Saturday night, Alice had appraised the situation coolly and said, "Ssccreeww this! We'll have our own party, won't we, girls?" And she'd dragged every woman in town off with her. They were all up at Alice's now, Rudy thought, and they weren't drinking whisky. The women...they ordered it and hoarded it...creme de menthe, creme de cacao, creme de every damn thing, Rudy thought bitterly. And that wasn't all, for there was even scotch, bourbon, wines red and white and all shades in between, vodka... They hoarded it and mingled and piled it together on a table, laughing, concocting recipes. From a distance about the size of an NHL hockey rink, the men imagined they could hear the women laughing.

Rudy lusted after their party. In his heart of hearts, that's where he wanted to be, not that he lusted after the women, but he lusted after the great goblets of multicoloured booze. Between plays, he sat and imagined them in their insular world, warm and uncaring about the cold silence of the night, the temperature falling dangerously. They probably had those little swizzle sticks with St. Pete's Beach pink and tangerine umbrellas in the glasses. They'd done it before; that's the sort of women they were.

Rudy stirred in his chair, the drink diminishing with every grimace. A great sadness sat upon him, and a restlessness. Oh, he wanted to go, wanted to get out of this room, the dank air that smelled like wet mittens. But where? The women were adamant about not letting the men in until the game was over. It was the punishment for the shut-ups long suffered through hockey games. There was nowhere to go, save the place where he was already. For an instant, he imagined Magda, and a sudden desire for a city a thousand miles away rose in him. So Rudy repeated his ritual, downed another drink, and having no place to go, headed for the ice.

Women, he thought as he sped through the snow past Alice's. The troubling vision of Magda was still with him, and as her face formed and reformed in the swirling snow, Rudy pondered the cruelty of women. Magda had banished him to this place, and those other women wouldn't let him into the party. No men until after midnight. By then, all the booze would be gone or hidden, and the drunken commingling of men and women would serve only to send the right or wrong couples home together. So Rudy rode over the ice, too tired to curse Wayne Gretzky and thus gain inclusion in the men's party, and barred by decree from the other.

Rudy thought of Magda now, as he always did when he was drunk. He couldn't avoid her when he was drunk, her neat well-fleshed figure, her light brown curls shaking in disbelief, her mouth constricted and disapproving...

"Your mouth...fuck, Magda...I hate it when you do that," he'd said. "I fuckin hate it...you pull it in and pucker it all up," he said, imitating her now, "...like a...likeaan...arsehole..."

"From living with one," she'd said.

And she'd gone out, leaving him there on the floor, a jester without an audience. And then what choice had he, what choice, as time and time again she cut him down, what choice but to seek out the guest room in Fred and Joan's dark basement, what choice but to find a way out of there too, what choice but to grab wildly for teaching jobs, and to take the first one that was offered, what choice but to go, go...

The skidoo buzzed powerfully, pleasantly in the darkness. He wasn't going fast. But he felt that he was flying. The heady buzz of the machine produced the illusion. Rudy flying ahead, ahead.

Rudy was allout for it tonight. He was going to the Shenak, a world that had grown in his mind, invented from the word, the idea—*sena,* going to see the seals raise their heads from the dark waters at the edge of the world of ice, and Rudy thought he would never see these seals but he would feel them around him and hear them breathe, and suddenly that was the thing he wanted.

Rudy gunned the machine, give her, give her, he thought, give her. On a straight, he freed a hand to take the flask out of his pocket, and pulled deeply. In the cold, cold, cold, the whisky was a pleasant fire, and the fire lulled him, and the machine lulled him and the night had no sounds, no sounds at all within it. And the Northern Lights did shimmery dances and if you got too close, they'd cut your head off, but they wouldn't get too close to Rudy because he was hunched over, face bent behind the windscreen which wavered and made lows and highs in the landscape where none existed, and Rudy drove on and the Northern Lights couldn't touch him because he was lying almost flat and as he moved through the night, he clenched his teeth and murmured give 'er, give 'er. And Rudy was racing, racing when the headlights dimmed to a dull orange, the engine sputtered and sputtered again, and died, shuddering a little like an animal in its own warmth. It stopped dead, and suddenly there was no sound, no light at all, only an infinite dark silence around him and he sat, feeling himself to be a ridiculous little man in the middle of nowhere with a dead machine between his legs.

As he usually did in emergencies, Rudy thought, "I'll have a drink first." A drink made the ghosts go away, a drink silenced Magda, a drink was what he needed right now. And thus he felt for his pocket. He couldn't see his pocket; his coat and the night had merged into one, a solidity of darkness. But he could see his gloves, light buff gauntlets, and it seemed to him that his hand, disembodied and ghostly, moved around his body, found his pocket, and came back of its own holding the flask.

He sucked back on the whisky. When he had a drink, the skidoo would start up again. He was inclined to believe at this moment that the skidoo was just like an animal and was tired, and would go on again bravely after it had had a rest. But this time he'd turn it around and point it home. "Fuckin fool," he cursed himself; "What the fuck did you think you were doing?"

And then through the fog of his drunkenness, it came to him; he was going to the Shenak, going to the edge of the ice to see the seals raise their smooth heads from the water at the edge of the ice. But the edge of the ice is the edge of the world, Rudy thought now, and if you did get there, you'd never get back. You're crazy, crazy, he told himself. It was a good thing, he thought that the skidoo had stopped.

Otherwise, he'd have gone on, God knows how far, and what would have happened then? He patted the hood of the skidoo affectionately, as if it were a friend who had just warned him of great danger. He walked around it, surprised that his legs were so weak from the vibrations of riding. Had he come so far, then? He pulled on the bottle.

What do I care, he thought, I'm here with friends; he patted the skidoo and he patted the bottle. And Rudy felt at that moment very cheerful.

But the bottle was nearly empty now. Rudy was surprised that he didn't feel really cold; there was no immediacy in his desire to return. Instead, he sat on the skidoo seat, the vinyl crackling as he sat on it, and drew in the night. The air burned his lungs and the whisky burned his throat. The sensations were sharp-edged, pleasantly angular and poignant. Sitting there, he tried whistling a small tune in praise of whisky, but his voice frightened him and the whistle died on his lips. One more drink, he thought...lots of time...then I'll go back.

He raised the bottle, and throwing his head back, drained it. Above him, the Northern Lights rippled like stage curtains, tessellations of shapes infinitely disintegrating and reforming, pink and green and a pale cold amethyst. A shooting star fell, and Rudy thought as he caught it out of the corner of his eye that he should wish on it. But what would he wish for...Magda...he thought foolishly. And then...I wish I was back at Eddy's... And this brought him to his present situation and the need to take some action.

The Shenak...seals...he thought, I must be crazy. But then in the darkness he thought he was there, and maybe he could have come so far without knowing, for if he squinted into the darkness, he thought he could see shapes rising and sinking around him but it was difficult, so dark that the exercise made him feel that his eyes were bulging clean out of his head. And yet…if he listened he thought that he could hear a creaking, a creaking that was the unearthly sound one hears at the edge of the ice, when the ice pitches and buckles from the strain of the great ocean heaving beneath it.

And Rudy told himself that the crackling was only the crackling of his nylon clothing as he moved, and the crackling of the stiff seat of the skidoo. But he was feeling frightened, and it came to him suddenly that he was procrastinating, that he hadn't tried to start the machine because maybe it wouldn't start, maybe he was stuck here.

And at that moment Rudy got up, staggered a little. I'm going home, he announced to himself.

He primed the skidoo, and gave the pulley four short hauls. But nothing happened. No sound of the engine springing into life, no throb, no lights pointing the way out of the darkness. I'll try again, he thought. And then again. But no sound, no lights emerged out of the darkness and silence.

He reached to prime it again and then in a flash of clarity thought, Jesus, I've flooded the engine, and there was no cure for that but rest. Rudy didn't search for his tool-kit. He knew where it was, home in the closet in the porch. Dumb *Kudlanak*, he cursed himself for not bringing it.

And then from feeling that he had gone all the way to the edge of the ice, Rudy thought that no, he was very close to town, very close indeed, and hadn't he been riding for only a little while? And he was sure that if he walked for a bit, he'd round the curve of the bay and see the lights of the town strung out and welcoming. Sure he would. And Eddy and the boys would be up at Alice MacKay's. He'd go up there for a drink.

So Rudy walked. And he tried to hum silently to himself as he didn't like the sound of his voice when it left him. It seemed to meet with a great solidity a few inches from him, and bounced back to him, obscenely loud. So he hummed silently, thankful now for the clothing he'd paid a small fortune for at

Eddy Bauer, because it really did keep him warm; he couldn't, in fact, feel any cold at all. So Rudy walked on, warm inside his warm clothes, the nylon of his pants making rhythmic sounds as they came together in a regular stride in the direction from which he'd originally come.

And, still drunk, he couldn't banish Magda completely as she slipped into the space vacated by his useless worry, but he was grateful for her presence now. In fact, he found himself talking to her, telling her that he'd always known that when the time came that he really needed her, she'd be there. Magda, he thought, Magda who always found jobs when there were none. Magda who kept him in school, Magda who was fed up with his frigging intellectual friends, and the late hours and the drinking. And here she was, closer, infinitely more real than she'd been on the journey out. Rudy didn't care now; he was bawling, sobbing, asking her to forgive him, Magda, please...please...he begged, entreating her to forgive his sins, his wild drinking of their money, his sharp mocking tongue when she complained, the roomful of paper that even after three years...three years...had never materialized as a thesis...

And she was forgiving him. Nodding and smiling, she understood; she was forgiving him. And she was walking beside him, wasn't she, not minding the cold or his foolish bawling, and Rudy felt warm and content as they walked toward the town, the rhythmic crunch of snow-pants making its little sound. The Northern Lights shimmered only inches above their heads as they walked away from the seals at the edge of the world of ice, away from the Shenak.

March 29

I have been dreaming about fruit again. Last night I walked through a market. Stalls poured out fresh fruit, grapes spilled off tables. There was a rich fermenting smell; burst melons lay in the street. I filled a basket and sat eating strawberries; they were so real I woke up with their sweetness in my mouth.

Then, while I was stuffing myself, I had the feeling I was being watched. Derek appeared wearing a load of bananas on his head. He looked like Carmen Miranda. He handed me a letter edged in black. He said it was from home.

Slight hangover. Women's party at Alice's last night. Maybe it was Alice's tropical punch that brought on the fruit dream. We were all talking about spring, with the drapes closed against the frigid night. Yesterday afternoon the sun was so strong that you could feel its heat on your shoulders, and even though the unseasonal heat gave way to one of the coldest nights we've had in a long time, you could tell that everyone had been cheered up, made hopeful by the brief heat. Alice says that June is a beautiful month, with late-night sunsets and hardly any real darkness at all.

What a bore Sunday is. I just lie here until some necessity gets me up.

Of course, I have lots of letters of application to write. So I am flinging them far and wide, casting them out, hoping they will catch something — anything — in their net. I just got one of those wonderful booklets you can send away for — an international listing of job vacancies.

I see myself on a beach somewhere where all the place names sound like the names of cocktails.

Santa ... something.

Away in the sun, the magical south.